"I'm here to collect my woman..."

Lily blinked.

Fletcher regarded her with exaggerated patience. "What have I told you about chasing other guys?" he demanded, as unamused by her antics as she was by his.

"Nothing," Lily said, enunciating as if to a dunce. And truly, Fletcher was acting like one.

Fletcher gave Carson a man-to-man glance. "What can I say?" he apologized. "She likes the chase—" Fletcher reached out and tugged Lily off the sofa "—and I like giving her one." Behaving as if he had some right to be going all possessive on her, Fletcher swept her off her feet.

The assistant held the door open for him and Fletcher carried Lily down the steps. While everyone—the townspeople, cast and crew, directors and producers—looked on with unbridled interest, Fletcher paused.

And, still holding her cradled in his arms, slowly and ardently lowered his head to hers.

"Don't. You. Dare," Lily said.

But of course, Fletcher did.

Dear Reader,

Life is full of contradictions, and so are people. For instance, we all have a public side—how we are perceived by those who don't know anything about us except for what they see. And we all have a private side—the person we are when we are relaxed and at ease, in the company of those we love and trust.

Florist Lily Madsen was reared to be the perfect Southern lady, and although part of her is just that, Lily also has a secret, ultra-sexy, all-grown-up side that is, after years of way too much heartache for someone her age, just rarin' to break free.

Veterinarian Fletcher Hart is known to be the most savvy—and deeply cynical—of all Helen Hart's sons. Reckless and restless, the dedicated healer has a reputation for never letting anyone get too close.

At first glance, a worse love match could never be made. Which is why Fletcher resolves to stay as far away as possible from the sweet and lovely Lily. Fletcher has enough on his conscience without adding the "corruption" of the naively innocent Lily to the list.

The only problem is, headstrong Lily is about to get herself in a heap of trouble. And Fletcher just can't let that happen. Even if it means casting himself in the unfamiliar role of hero-to-the-rescue, making all her dreams come true and seducing her instead!

I hope you enjoy Fletcher and Lily's love story as much as I enjoyed writing it. For more information on this and my other books, you can visit me at www.cathygillenthacker.com.

Best wishes,

Cathy Gillen Thacker

Cathy Gillen Thacker

THE
SECRET
SEDUCTION

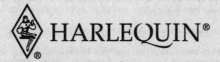

TORONTO • NEW YORK • LONDON
AMSTERDAM • PARIS • SYDNEY • HAMBURG
STOCKHOLM • ATHENS • TOKYO • MILAN • MADRID
PRAGUE • WARSAW • BUDAPEST • AUCKLAND

ISBN 0-373-75026-9

THE SECRET SEDUCTION

Copyright © 2004 by Cathy Gillen Thacker.

This edition published by arrangement with Harlequin Books S.A.

® and TM are trademarks of the publisher. Trademarks indicated with ® are registered in the United States Patent and Trademark Office, the Canadian Trade Marks Office and in other countries.

www.eHarlequin.com

Printed in U.S.A.

Chapter One

Honestly, Lily Madsen thought as she watched the disheveled "cowboy" climb down from the truck, that man in the snug-fitting jeans, chambray shirt and boots was enough to take your breath away. Or he would have been, she amended, if he hadn't been Fletcher Hart. The most reckless and restless of Helen Hart's five sons, the thirty-year-old Fletcher had a reputation for loving and leaving women and never committing to much of anything—save his thriving Holly Springs, North Carolina, vet practice—for long.

"Why are you being so all-fired difficult?" Lily glared at him and continued the conversation the two of them had started before Fletcher had cut it short and headed off on an emergency call to a nearby farm. "All I am asking for is a simple introduction to Carson McRue. I'll take it the rest of the way."

"I'm sure you will." Fletcher slanted her a deeply cynical look, followed it with a way too knowing half smile, then strode toward the back door of the clinic, all confident indomitable male. "The answer is still no, Lily."

Simmering with a mixture of resentment, anger and another emotion she couldn't quite identify, Lily followed Fletcher into the building, aware that unlike the building, which smelled quite antiseptic, he smelled as if he had been rolling around in the back of a barn. And perhaps he had been, she thought, noting the sweat stains on his shirt, the mud clinging to his backside, knees, shoulders and chest.

Oblivious to her scrutiny of him, he strode purposefully into a glass-walled room. On the other side of the partition was an assortment of cats and dogs in metal cages. All appeared to be recovering from operations or illness and were sleeping or resting drowsily. On their side of the glass wall, there was another large crate with a dog inside who did not appear to have had surgery.

Lily watched as Fletcher hunkered down beside the crate and peered in. To her frustration, he seemed a lot more interested in his canine patient, than what she had to say to him. "Just what is your objection to my meeting the man anyway?" she demanded with all the authority she could muster, given the five years' difference in their ages.

Fletcher paused to give a comforting pat to the ailing yellow lab, who looked up at him with big sad eyes, before straightening once again. "Besides the fact that he's an egotistical TV star who doesn't care about anyone but himself, you mean?" Fletcher challenged.

Lily huffed her exasperation and folded her arms in front of her, trying all the while not to notice how soft and touchable Fletcher's shaggy honey-brown hair was, how sexy his golden-brown eyes. You would think the way Fletcher acted that he was the star of a hit TV show, instead of a local vet who was—as always—in need of a haircut. Just because he had a masculine chiseled face, with the don't-mess-with-me Hart jaw, expressive, kissable lips, a strong nose and well-defined cheekbones, did not mean that she had to swoon at his feet. And the same went for his powerful, six-foot-one frame, with those broad shoulders, impossibly solid chest, lean waist and long, muscular legs.

"You don't know that for sure," she retorted defensively, privately hoping it wasn't true. "Just because Carson McRue is rich and famous—"

Fletcher headed up the stairs that led to his apartment on the second floor, unbuttoning his filthy shirt as he went. Lily was right behind him. "Let's just cut the bull, shall we?"

"I don't—"

He stopped at the top of the stairs and stripped off his shirt, leaving Lily with a bird's-eye view of lots of satiny smooth male skin, a T-shaped mat of golden-brown hair, six-pack abs and a belly button so sexy it was to die for. With effort, she dragged her glance away from his hip-hugging jeans and American Veterinary Medical Association belt buckle, before she could really give in to temptation and slide her glance lower to see what was behind that tightly shut zipper.

Oblivious to the licentious direction of her thoughts, Fletcher continued mocking her with thinly veiled contempt. "I know about the bet you made with all your friends. Okay, Lily? Everyone in town does.''

While Fletcher watched, embarrassed color crept to her cheeks. Lily gulped her dismay. She never should have indulged in such bold talk at her birthday party last week. But then she never should have let her friends talk her into having two margaritas with her enchiladas, either. Everyone knew she couldn't hold her liquor. The closest she had ever gotten to drinking was the smidgen of crème de menthe her grandmother had let them have in their milk every Christmas Eve.

Alcohol had been one of many things her beloved grandmother Rose had not approved. And knowing how badly her own parents had disappointed Grandmother Rose, Lily had grown up never wanting to similarly let her down.

Forcing herself to meet Fletcher's boldly assessing gaze head-on, Lily demanded archly, ''Who told you—?'' And more to the point, how much exactly did he know about what she had sworn she would do to win her wager?

''—That you've promised when Carson McRue's private jet leaves Carolina, you're going to be on it?'' Fletcher picked up where Lily left off. ''Well, let's see. There's my sister, Janey. My brother Joe's wife, Emma. Hannah Reid, over at Classic Car Auto Repair. My cousin Susan Hart. And everyone else who heard you swear that you could get a hot date with the dim bulb in just one week.''

Fletcher Hart knew everything, all right. Except of course what had prompted Lily to make such an unlikely, hedonistic boast in the first place. She pushed her rebuttal through gritted teeth. "Carson McRue is not a dim bulb. Or an egotistical star."

That cynical smile again. "And how would you know this?" Fletcher challenged as he unlocked the door and strode into his apartment, past the messy living room, kitchen and bedroom, to the bathroom at the rear.

Lily had the choice of following, or cooling her heels. She knew what he would have preferred, and—feeling stubbornly contrary—did the exact opposite. Pulse racing, she leaned against the hallway wall with her back to the open bathroom door and continued their conversation as nonchalantly as if every single day she did things this intimate with men she barely knew. "I know because I've watched his TV show every week for the last five years." The action-adventure show about an easygoing Hollywood private eye had been the one bright spot in many a stressful week. Lily had watched the highly entertaining program in hospital rooms and waiting rooms, as well as at home. And it had never failed to make her forget her problems, at least temporarily. Right now she needed to forget her problems. Besides, if she won her bet with the girls, they all owed her a day at the spa. If she lost and they won, well, Lily didn't want to think about what she would have to do then. Especially since Fletcher didn't seem to know about the price she would have to pay, either. Otherwise she was sure he would have already rudely brought it up.

Fletcher kicked off one boot, then the other. "Carson McRue plays a character, Lily. What you see on TV is all an act, albeit a highly polished one.''

''I know that,'' Lily retorted drolly as she heard a zip and a whoosh of fabric…and *was that the shower starting?* Telling herself she was not going to see Fletcher naked, no matter how brazenly he was behaving, she closed her eyes and rubbed at the tense spot just above her nose.

''But no one who isn't that nice could actually pretend to be that caring and compassionate.'' At least Lily hoped that was the case. Otherwise, her goose was cooked. She would never be able to live down this drunken boast. Never be able to get up the nerve to do what she had to do to make good on her lost wager…

''Don't count on it,'' Fletcher argued right back. ''And anyway, it doesn't matter.'' The shower curtain opened and closed. Water pelted in an entirely different rhythm and the aroma of soap and shampoo and…man…wafted out on the steamy air as Fletcher scrubbed himself clean. ''I'm still not introducing you to him.'' He spoke above the din of running water.

At Fletcher's stubbornness, it was all Lily could do not to stomp her foot. ''But he and the rest of the show's cast and crew will be here tomorrow,'' she protested hotly as he shut the water off, pulled open the shower curtain with a telltale whoosh and ripped a towel off the rack with equal carelessness. ''And you're the only one in town who has met him.''

Six heavy male footsteps later, Fletcher was standing in the hall. Knowing she would be a coward if she didn't look, Lily opened her eyes. Fletcher was standing there, regarding her curiously and unabashedly. He had a towel slung low around his waist. He was using another on his hair. And, she noticed disconcertingly, he looked every bit as deliciously sexy wet as he did dry.

"I found the guy a horse to ride while he's here. That's it. And all that required was a phone call and video-conference," Fletcher told Lily in disdain.

That was far more contact than anyone else in town had had, Lily thought enviously. Why didn't anything that exciting ever happen to her? And if it didn't, how was she ever going to leave her Ice Princess of Holly Springs reputation far behind?

"You're also going to be working at the set, as the animal-rights consultant." She diligently made her case for him to help her.

Fletcher shrugged his broad shoulders, and Lily's pulse picked up as she saw the loosely knotted towel around his waist slip a little bit.

Fletcher frowned, unimpressed. "It's a glorified title. I only took the position because of the hefty paycheck attached to it. It doesn't mean I really have any say in what goes on there. Unless of course they try to do some stunt that would actually harm any of the animals on the set. And right now, the only animal I know about is the horse Carson McRue will be riding when he takes off after the bad guys."

"Fine. Whatever." Lily did not care if Fletcher ended up being bored out of his mind. "The point is, the film crew is only going to be here for one week and you've got entrée. And I do have a bet going…''

Fletcher met her eyes, this time in all seriousness. "One that is bound to guarantee you getting hurt."

Lily's spine stiffened. She wished like heck that he would behave more modestly or put some clothes on. Not that she could actually see anything she shouldn't be seeing…or wouldn't see if he were, say, swimming.

"You don't know that," she retorted defensively in an attempt to get her mind off of what was under that towel. Was that as gloriously male and wonderfully attractive as the rest of him? And how would she—the woman of literally no worldly experience—know anyway, even if she were to see? She'd never encountered a naked man! Except on the big screen and in the movies she'd seen. And it was always a rear view, never ever the front.

"Don't I?" Fletcher let go of the towel he had looped around his neck. He flattened a hand on the wall next to her and leaned in close, deliberately invading her space. "Let's recap for a moment here, shall we?" he said softly. "Small-town girl—that would be you—who has never been out of Holly Springs, except for that one half semester she went to college in Winston-Salem before returning to finish up her studies at nearby N.C. State, tries to hook up with a Hollywood hunk who has a reputation for breaking hearts all over the world."

Lily did not need reminding how stifling her life to date had been. "First of all, Fletcher," she retorted, lifting her chin, "it was never my decision to live my whole life in North Carolina or live at home while I finished my business degree. But I had no choice. My grandmother was ill—and someone had to be there to drive her to medical appointments and see her through the surgeries, radiation and chemo-therapy treatments.'' Lily gulped around the sudden tightness in her throat. ''So I did it, and further-more—'' her voice quavered even more as she thought about the heartbreak of that awful time ''—I was glad to do it.''

Fletcher's eyes softened and he touched a gentle hand to her quivering chin. ''I know that,'' he told her compassionately. ''I'm sorry you lost her. You know how much I cared about Grandmother Rose. And the pets she had over the years.''

Lily did know. An animal lover from birth, Fletcher knew everyone in town, and their pets. His future as a veterinarian had seemed as predetermined as Lily's, who had been tapped to continue the florist business that had been in the Madsen family for gen-erations. The difference being Fletcher had gone into his career by choice. Lily had been forced into hers by duty. And at twenty-five, after years of sacrifice, she was getting pretty darned tired of doing what *everyone else* felt she should.

''Which is why, Lily, I and everyone else in this town who care about you do not want to see you make a fool out of yourself over an arrogant thes-pian.''

''Don't you think that should be my choice?'' Lily tapped him on the chest before she could think—then withdrew her index finger from that warm, hard chest and leaned back as far as she could into the wall.

Fletcher's eyes grew dark, as he stayed right where he was. "Not if you're going to make the wrong decision, no," he said flatly. "I don't."

"WHAT IN THE TARNATION did you do to that little filly?" Fletcher's brother Dylan asked, tongue in cheek, an hour later. A TV sportscaster by profession, Dylan couldn't seem to stop observing and commenting on everything around him, even when he wasn't working. But then, Fletcher noted, that was all Dylan had always been—a "watcher" rather than a "doer." Whereas Fletcher could have cared less what anyone else—save the delectable Lily Madsen—was up to as long as it didn't directly impact him.

"I don't know what you're talking about," Fletcher said, happy that his sister Janey was getting married to a man who deserved her, but wishing Janey and Thad Lantz had selected any other night for their wedding week kickoff pig pickin' in his mother's backyard.

Fletcher's oldest brother Mac, looking as much a lawman out of uniform as in, edged closer, a plate of pork barbecue in his hand. "Lily Madsen hasn't stopped glaring at you since the two of you walked in together."

Fletcher forked up some of his own shredded pork and tangy barbecue sauce, irked because they were treating his coming in with the stubborn minx as if it were some sort of date, and it darn well wasn't.

"I didn't ask her to the party," Fletcher said, exasperated. "So don't go making anything out of us coming in together." That was just the way it had happened, thanks to Lily's refusal to give up on her pitch right until the minute they walked in here side by side.

"Yeah, we know." The twenty-eight-year-old Dylan winked.

Cal continued with a salacious grin. "At least *she* was on time."

Fletcher shrugged his shoulders helplessly. Cal might have been the first of them to get married, but his wife Ashley's current OB/GYN fellowship in Honolulu had him living the everyday life of a single man again. And though Cal kept insisting it wasn't a marital separation, it looked to everyone else in the family as if it were. Particularly since it had been going on for two years now.

Not that Cal had ever looked at another woman. Ashley was—and always would be—the love of Cal's life. For all the good it did him, Fletcher noted cynically.

"I couldn't help being late." Fletcher finally answered the charge against him. "A sick cow needed my attention."

"No problem. Lily Madsen was only too happy to volunteer to go and find you and drag you over here." Cal continued teasing, even as the beeper on his belt went off, signaling a message regarding one of his orthopedic patients.

Fletcher guzzled his icy cold beer as Cal stepped away to use his cell to phone the hospital. "Can I

help it if I'm not much for parties these days?"
Fletcher asked.

"Who are you kidding?" Joe razzed, looking fit
as a fiddle, even in the Carolina Storm hockey team's
off-season as he chowed down on liberal amounts of
coleslaw, beans and shredded pork. "You've never
been much for parties. Always too busy tending to
some sick or wounded animal."

Fletcher wasn't going to apologize for his devotion
to his work. He plucked a golden brown hush puppy
off his plate. "That's my job."

Thad Lantz, Janey's fiancé, joined the group. "Not
twenty-four hours a day, seven days a week," Thad
said with the same frank authority he used as coach
of the Carolina Storm hockey team. "You've got a
partner. She takes calls from time to time. Or so I've
heard."

"And your point is?" Fletcher asked Thad.

"It's best to play as hard as you work."

And all he needed, Fletcher thought sardonically,
was a playmate who didn't want hearts and flowers
and marriage—or anything else he was ill equipped
to give.

Even as he thought it a single woman came to
mind. Beautiful, blond and all of twenty-five...

"I think we're getting off subject here," Dylan
said, guiding the conversation back to where it began. He looked at Fletcher curiously. "We want to
know what you did or said to Lily Madsen to get her
so ticked off at you."

Fletcher turned and looked at Lily. She was deep
in conversation with his mother and sister, and the

other bridesmaids. And she looked absolutely gorgeous. Like the cherubic angel he remembered her being as a kid, and yet…all grown up. Definitely grown up. Her five-foot-five frame was slender but curvy in all the right places, her legs stunning enough to make even the most jaded guy stop and take a second and third look. Her baby-blond curls had been cut to chin-length, but these days she wore them in a tousled, unconsciously sexy, finger-combed style that drove him wild. Her soft pink bow-shaped lips had a sensual slant and the rest of her features—the straight slender nose, high cheekbones, wide-set Carolina blue eyes—were elegance defined.

She was incredibly feminine, and it didn't matter whether she was wearing the khaki pants and pastel T-shirts he sometimes spotted her in, or the kind of floaty, flirty tea-length floral sundress and high-heeled sandals she had on now. She always exuded a sort of purity and innocence that was amazing for someone her age, especially in this day and age. Which was why, Fletcher thought as Lily turned and sent a brief, dagger-filled look his way, he had to stay away from her. Which probably wouldn't be hard, given all the reasons he had just given her to absolutely loathe and detest him.

Reluctantly, he broke off their staring match and turned back to Thad and his brothers. Aware they were still waiting for an explanation, he said, "She wants me to fix her up with Carson McRue when he hits town tomorrow to start filming *Hollywood P.I.*"

"And you refused?" Mac guessed dryly.

Hell, yes, he had refused, Fletcher thought as he

took another swig of his beer. "Lily is much too innocent to be hooked up with a narcissist like McRue," Fletcher said in the most disaffected tone he could manage.

"Let me guess. You gave her a hard time about wanting to go out with him at all," Cal said.

"No," Fletcher replied, beginning to feel exasperated again as Lily shot him another withering look over her shoulder, which was followed by a whole slew of withering looks from his mother and the other bridesmaids. "I simply told her the way it was," Fletcher continued matter-of-factly, defending his actions. "And I wouldn't have done that if she had just taken my hint and not asked for my assistance in garnering an introduction."

The male members of the wedding party turned to look at the female participants. Especially Lily, who still looked awfully ticked off, like her temper was sky-high. "What'd you say to her?" Dylan asked curiously.

That was just it. Fletcher could hardly recall—he had been so focused on Lily and that sexy lilac perfume she was wearing.

Fletcher swallowed around the sudden dryness in his throat as he pushed away memories of just how kissable her pink and pouty lips had been, how silken her peaches and cream skin. "I just wasn't very helpful."

Joe smirked. "Not being helpful usually doesn't earn you razor-sharp looks like that." Since getting hooked up with his wife, Emma, earlier in the summer, the pro athlete in the family suddenly considered himself an expert on all things female. "So what'd you do?" Joe prodded.

I got into a shower in front of her, in hopes of scaring her away. Unfortunately, Fletcher admitted remorsefully to himself, it hadn't worked. And now, all Fletcher could remember was Lily's eyes roving over him as her face flushed and her breathing grew shallow. And he wondered what it would be like to see her in—and just out—of the shower.

"Have we been missing something here?" Mac leaned in closer. His work as sheriff had trained him to notice absolutely everything. "Have you two got something going on?"

"Nope." Fletcher said honestly as Lily sent him yet another heated look. And just as suddenly, inspiration hit. Fletcher caught and held Lily's eyes until she finally blushed and turned away with a haughty snap of her head. "But we just might," he drawled.

Dylan scoffed. "Fat chance, considering she's got her eyes on another prize."

Fletcher had never taken well to disrespect. He wasn't going to start now. He finished the last of the barbecue on his plate. "You think I can't do it?"

"Win her attentions?" Mac sopped up the last of his barbecue sauce with a piece of sourdough bread. "You bet."

Fletcher set his plate and bottle of beer aside. "You're on."

Cal blinked, sure he had missed something. "What?"

Fletcher stepped closer and dropped his voice to a

husky whisper. "Hundred dollars says I can make Lily Madsen forget all about going out with Carson McRue."

Joe shook his head, predicting, "She'll never give up on a date with the hunk, if only because it'll mean losing the bet she made at her twenty-fifth birthday party last week."

It didn't matter to Fletcher. Not in the least. Or it wouldn't, when he was through waylaying Lily Madsen at every conceivable opportunity. "She'll do it," he boasted, to one and all, aiming his thumb at his chest. "In order to go out with me."

"WHAT WERE YOU and your brothers and future brother-in-law talking about for so long over there?" Lily demanded at the end of the party as Fletcher prepared to drive her home. The palatial, three-story white brick Wedding Inn that Fletcher's mother ran loomed across the manicured lawns.

"Nothing that concerns you," Fletcher fibbed.

All four of his brothers and Thad had wanted in on the action. With five hundred dollars riding on his wager—and his secret deathbed promise to Lily's grandmother spurring him on—Fletcher had powerful incentive to keep Lily from being hurt by Carson McRue.

She looked him up and down, color flooding her face. Feeling an answering heat well up deep inside him, he yearned to throw convention aside and simply take her in his arms and kiss her, if only to stop whatever it was she was going to say to him next. "I don't believe you," she said quietly.

Fletcher shrugged and folded his arms in front of his broad chest. ''If you must know,'' he continued lazily, standing with his shoulders back, legs braced apart, ''they were razzing me about the dirty looks you gave me all during the pig-picking.''

Just as he had expected, the attitude he was exuding only served to infuriate her all the more. ''Did you tell them what a cad you were?'' she demanded with a haughty toss of her head, looking all Southern belle, born and bred.

Didn't have to. They had guessed as much, and of course, he already knew. Which was another reason, Fletcher figured, it would be best if Lily continued to detest him, both before and after he won his bet, of course. He needed to convince her once and for all she needed to hold out for someone far better than either him or Carson McRue to come along and sweep her off her feet and give her the kind of life she deserved.

''Well, then,'' Fletcher said, taking an astonished Lily into his arms and bringing her shockingly close as he prepared to give her something to really loathe him for, ''I guess it's high time I lived up to my 'reputation.' Don't you?''

Chapter Two

Lily couldn't believe it. Fletcher Hart was actually going to kiss her. Right here as the party was breaking up, in front of everyone getting into their cars. "I don't—" she said, splaying her hands across his warm, hard chest. Before she could protest further, his lips were on hers, and in one sizzling instant, all reasonable thought left her brain and she was only aware of the sensations rippling through her. The smooth lips. Seductive pressure. The incredibly good taste of his lips and mouth and tongue as he erotically deepened and took full command of the kiss. She'd heard about embraces like this, read about them, even seen them when a few of her friends fell head over heels in love with the men of their dreams, but never had she experienced anything like the tumultuous whirlwind of emotion and pleasure.

And even though she knew, in some distant part of her brain, that Fletcher was only doing this to provoke her, the fun-and-pleasure-starved part of it never wanted it to end. Because fiery hot kisses like this, men who could kiss like this, so masterfully and evocatively, did not come along every day. As his arms wrapped all the tighter around her, and he brought her even closer to his hard, demanding length, Lily moaned, surprising herself with the sensuality of her response, and melted deeper into the embrace. And that was when she heard it—the low male laughter surrounding them.

The sound was like a bucket of ice water being dumped on her head. She broke off the impetuous kiss and looked around to see Fletcher's brothers chuckling and shaking their heads with a mixture of amusement and chastisement.

"Getting a head start there?" Dylan remarked sarcastically.

"You better watch yourself," Mac warned as he strolled to the SUV he drove whenever he wasn't on duty as the Holly Springs sheriff.

Joe sauntered past, his wife Emma's hand tucked in his. "You could find yourself married before you know it."

Joe sure had, Lily remembered, thinking of the whirlwind romance earlier in the summer that now had Joe and Emma living as man and wife.

Despite the odds against a happily-ever-after in the situation Joe and Emma had initially found themselves in, Lily had to admit the two looked very happy now.

"Ah, leave him alone," Cal said, waving off the interference of their other brothers. "It was only a kiss. Kisses don't mean anything." Cal turned his attention to her, looking every bit the compassionate doctor he was known to be. "Right, Lily?"

"In this case, definitely right," Lily confirmed

stormily, trying to look as casual as if she did things like this every day when everyone knew she did not.

"From where I was standing it looked like Lily was kissing him back. And that does mean something," Thad said, as he leaned over to buss his bride-to-be's cheek. "Right, Janey?"

"That's where all my troubles started." Janey sighed, looking as happy as any engaged woman should be as she laced her arm around Thad's waist and leaned her cheek against his chest.

"It's all disgusting to me," her 12-year-old son, Christopher, said, as he tagged along behind his mother and Thad.

"Not to worry," Lily said, glaring at Fletcher. "It's not going to happen again." She hurried to catch up with his older brother Mac. "Care to see me to my car?" she asked as she fell into his protective shadow.

"Be happy to, Lily." Mac flashed her a reassuring smile before turning to send his third oldest brother a censuring look. "And not to worry, Lily. You're safe with me."

UNFORTUNATELY, FLETCHER noticed right away, Lily was *not* going to be safe with the TV actor who rolled into town the following morning in a custom-outfitted silver trailer.

"Who's the beauty?" Carson McRue asked as he and Fletcher met to discuss a horse.

Fletcher followed Carson's glance. It led straight to Lily, who was loitering on the other side of the wooden barricades erected to keep the cast and crew of *Hollywood P.I.* away from the spectators gathering to watch the action in the town square.

Damned if Lily didn't look particularly gorgeous this morning, with her tousled blond hair and her sunglasses propped on top of her head. That pale pink sundress she was wearing not only hugged her slender curves to sexy advantage, it made her look like a peach blossom, ripe for the picking. Fletcher did his best to contain his mounting frustration. Protecting the headstrong and way-too-naive-for-her-own-good Lily from heartbreak was going to be no easy task. Especially with her constantly trying to win the bet she'd made with the girls. Fletcher's only comfort was that the bet he had made was—unlike hers—strictly under wraps to those who had made it with him.

He turned back to Carson, irked by the man's crassness in everything they discussed. His true personality seemed directly at odds with the great guy he played on TV. "She's off-limits," Fletcher stated casually.

Carson lifted a well-plucked brow. "Married?"

"Just off-limits," Fletcher repeated, doing his best to appeal to the actor's sensitive side. Assuming he had one. "Her grandmother, who was her only family, died last year. And she lost the cat she'd had since she was five years old, too. She had a very rough time."

Carson eyed Lily rapaciously, his glance lingering on her hourglass of curves. He licked his lips. "She looks ready to kick up her heels to me."

Punching out the competition would get him nowhere, Fletcher reminded himself firmly. At least right now. Later, if Carson continued in his current vein, all bets were off. "If you're looking for...companionship," Fletcher said meaningfully, "I can direct you to some likely places in Raleigh, Durham or Chapel Hill." There were dozens of bars in all three college towns. Lots of willing young women who would give anything to spend an evening in the handsome celebrity's company.

"No thanks. I like small-town girls." Carson continued studying Lily as if she were an item he'd like to purchase. "There's a sweetness and a purity about 'em. Besides, you never know...you could be giving one of them the thrill of a lifetime."

"And then what?" Fletcher asked.

Carson looked at Fletcher as if he were an infant, and not a particularly bright one at that. "We both move on." Carson spoke slowly and directly.

Only Fletcher knew Lily wouldn't be able to move on. Were she to be seduced and abandoned by someone like Carson McRue, it would crush her vulnerable heart.

"About the horse," Fletcher said impatiently, eager to have this business finished so he could go waylay Lily again and keep her from winning the wager.

Carson frowned his displeasure. "It's the wrong color."

It was Fletcher's turn to scowl. "You asked for a roan stallion—"

"I wanted a lighter brown," Carson interrupted, running a hand through his dark brown hair. "Something with a lot more copper in its coat. This one is too close to the color of my hair.''

Fletcher would have thought the actor was kidding if not for the earnestness on Carson's face.

''I'll see what I can do,'' Fletcher allowed, with as much professionalism as he could muster, ''but stunt horses are in short supply in this area of the country. And since you didn't want to pay to have one shipped in from the West Coast—''

''Just find what we need,'' Carson cut him off. ''I'm expert enough to ride even an untrained horse. And while you're at it—'' he pointed to a shady area, half a block away ''—do something about those two dogs over there.''

Fletcher turned and looked at the beagle mix and black Lab, sitting side by side in the shade, watching all the activity along with everyone else. ''They don't seem to be bothering anyone.''

''I'm allergic,'' Carson announced tightly.

Good to know, Fletcher thought.

''I don't want them barking and ruining a shot. We're going to be *filming* here later.'' Carson glared at Fletcher.

''Right.'' He nodded as if this were part of his job description.

''So call whomever you have to call and get rid of them,'' Carson continued.

''I'll try their owners,'' Fletcher said dryly.

Carson dismissed Fletcher and without a backward glance at any of the fans waving autograph books and calling his name, stepped inside his silver trailer.

Unbeknownst to him, Lily had somehow sweet-talked her way past the security guards standing watch over the barricades and was already heading toward them. She looked disappointed to have missed her chance to wangle an introduction out of Fletcher while Fletcher was talking to Carson. "Hoping to say hello?" he razzed her as she approached, wishing she didn't look quite so much like a Southern beauty queen this morning.

"Something like that." Lily looked past him, toward the door of Carson's trailer.

Fletcher moved to bar her path to the door and stood, legs braced apart, arms crossed in front of him. "Carson McRue specifically requested he not be disturbed," Fletcher informed Lily with a stern look.

Lily sighed, disappointed. "Maybe later," she hoped out loud.

Not if Fletcher had anything to do with it. Figuring, however, that Lily would not believe him even if he told her what Carson had just said about her, Fletcher let the opportunity to set her straight about the actor's true character pass. He gestured toward the two dogs chasing each other on the green. "Want to help me round those two up?" he asked her casually.

Lily's full lower lip slid out into a delectable pout. "I'm not a dog person. You know that."

Fletcher could imagine she didn't want to get her pale pink sundress dirty, and he couldn't really blame her. It looked expensive. Too expensive to be wasted on a guy like Carson McRue. "How do you know?" he challenged her playfully. "You've never owned a dog."

"So what are you hinting here, Fletcher? That dogs are superior to cats?" She looked down her nose at him. Clearly, she didn't think so.

"For a young single woman in need of protection—" *from men like Carson McRue,* Fletcher added silently "—yes. They are."

Lily lifted a delicate brow. "Maybe from know-it-alls like you," she acknowledged silkily.

Fletcher looked deep into her eyes, wishing he could haul her into his arms and kiss her senseless again. Just for the hell of it. But knowing that timing was everything, he forced himself to bide his time. He'd not only protect her when all was said and done, he'd win his bet, too. "Just come by the clinic later," Fletcher told Lily lazily and smiled as her cheeks pinkened all the more. "I'll introduce you to your new best friend," he promised.

"Don't hold your breath."

Fletcher merely kept smiling and didn't elaborate. If there was one thing he knew about Lily, she loved a good mystery, just like her grandmother Rose.

IT WAS JUST CURIOSITY, Lily told herself. That and the fact she had an order for a sumptuous bouquet to be delivered to the Holly Springs Animal Clinic reception desk at 6:00 p.m. The flowers were for the "staff" but none of the staff was there. Only the founding veterinarian, Fletcher Hart, who was looking mighty fine in a sage-green work shirt that nicely outlined his shoulders and powerful chest, and faded boot-cut jeans that did the same thing for his legs.

Fletcher came around the reception desk and took

the bouquet from her with a smile of thanks.
"They've all gone home."

Aware her pulse had picked up at the thought of
spending time alone with Fletcher—again—Lily
leaned against the counter and adapted the same lazy
insouciance he demonstrated. She watched him make
a big show of setting the flowers in a prominent place
on the large U-shaped desktop that fronted the reception area. "You placed this order, not Mr. N. L.
Spartacus."

"Well, he wanted to, but for obvious reasons he
couldn't contact the shop himself so I arranged it for
him."

"And sent that teenager in with a sealed envelope
of cash and instructions."

"What can I say?" Fletcher lifted his hands in a
mock gesture of helplessness. "The kid owed me a
favor."

"You are shameless," Lily accused sternly. And
sexy as could be, standing there, smelling of aftershave, his shaggy honey-brown hair all rumpled, and
the hint of evening beard on his masculine face. If
she didn't know better, she would think he was getting ready to go on a weeknight date, instead of
merely ending a workday.

His expressive lips tilted up in a playful half smile.
"I prefer to think of myself as a facilitator," he told
her wryly.

"I'll bet." Lily sighed, wishing she didn't recall
quite so acutely just how much fun it had been to
kiss him, even when the proud part of her said she
should have been slugging him a good one. She tilted

her head, wishing he didn't have a good eight inches on her in height. The disparity in their bodies made him seem all the more overwhelming. And she did not want to be taken over by Fletcher Hart, D.V.M. Setting her jaw, she forced herself to focus on the reason for her being there. "Why did Mr. N. L. Spartacus want to send the staff flowers, anyway?"

Fletcher appeared just as distracted as she was as he let his gaze rove over her hair, face and lips, before returning with laser accuracy to her eyes. "The usual," he said seriously. "N. L. Spartacus was grateful for the care he received here and wanted to show it."

"Mmm-hmm." Lily wasn't sure whether she was buying any of this or not. She narrowed her eyes at Fletcher. "And then you set it up so I had no choice but to bring the arrangement over myself." Thereby keeping her from pursuing her bet about Carson McRue. Not that she had been able to get anywhere near the actor that day, even when she wasn't working. Production company security had the area well blocked off. And Carson McRue, it seemed, was not acknowledging anyone but show personnel. At least for now....

"Hey!" Fletcher palmed his chest, caveman-style. "How was I to know you'd show up in person?"

"Because it's a well-known fact around town that all my part-time help goes home at 5:00 p.m. to cook dinner for their families. I always close."

"Okay. I admit N. L. Spartacus and I had an ulterior motive, getting you over here. And I'll show you what it is."

She looked at him blankly. He took her by the hand and led her into the room adjacent to the reception area. At the end in a big wire cage was the yellow Labrador retriever she had seen the previous day. He was lying down when they entered, but thumped his tail in greeting and looked up at them with hopeful eyes. It would have been enough to break Lily's heart, had she been a dog person. But she wasn't, she reassured herself firmly. And furthermore, didn't intend to be.

"Shouldn't you be talking to his owner?" she demanded crisply. She desperately did not want this to be her problem and she was afraid if she stayed here any longer it might very well be.

Fletcher reported in a flat, matter-of-fact voice, "His owner died four weeks ago. Spartacus—we've dubbed him N.L. because he Needs Love—was with the old guy when it happened. His owner was in his nineties and Spartacus stayed with him from the time he had the heart attack until he was found by a neighbor, three days later."

Lily caught her breath at the horror of the circumstances. "Oh, no." The poor thing....

"Anyway," Fletcher continued, his voice a little more gravelly, "Spartacus just went nuts when they tried to take the old guy away. He just wasn't going to let it happen. So the animal control people were summoned. Spartacus got one whiff of the truck that was going to take him to the pound and knew it wasn't for him, so he broke loose and ran off."

Lily pressed a hand to her heart. Her eyes were brimming with tears. "Then what happened?" she asked, the tragedy of the situation almost overwhelming her.

Fletcher shook his head, a brooding look coming into his eyes. "No one really knows. Three days ago, Spartacus showed up again at the house where he used to live, vomiting and so weak he could barely stand. This time the neighbors called my clinic, asked me to treat him. So I got in my pickup and went out to get him."

Lily looked back at Spartacus. "Needs Love" was certainly appropriate. She had never seen a dog with such a sad and lonely expression. If only he weren't so big. And strong looking. If only he were a cat. Cats, she knew. And yet he had his own appeal in that handsome big-dog way. His thick short fur was a pale, almost white-gold, and there was a stripe of darker gold down the center of his back that matched the color of his ears. On impulse, Lily hunkered down and reached out to touch him through the wires on the cage. She could feel his ribs sticking out prominently as she stroked his belly. She wondered how he had survived on his own for four weeks. She looked up at Fletcher as Spartacus leaned over to nuzzle the back of her palm affectionately with his black nose. "What was wrong with him?" she asked, still trying like heck not to get emotionally involved here, as his whiskers tickled her skin.

Fletcher shrugged, his emotions as tightly under wraps as hers were on the surface. "My guess is the canine equivalent of severe food poisoning. I think he'd been eating out of garbage cans while he was on the lam and got something particularly nasty, which isn't surprising in the summer heat. Bacteria grows like wildfire. Anyway, he's on the mend now, and I've got to find a new home for him.'' The playful grin was back on Fletcher's face as their eyes meshed again. ''I spoke to him about it this morning and he told me he kind of fancied the pretty blonde who had been in here hassling me yesterday, so I promised N.L. I'd propose pet adoption to you.''

Very funny. And designed to pull on my heartstrings. ''He can't talk,'' Lily pointed out.

''Come on.'' Fletcher assumed the boldly enthusiastic tone of an aggressive salesperson. ''Look at those big brown eyes and tell me you don't know what he's thinking.''

That was the problem—Lily did. And it was breaking her heart to admit she was not the person for the job. A dog like Spartacus needed someone knowledgeable in canine care. Telling herself it was for the best, Lily turned away. ''Have you talked to his previous neighbors?'' she asked.

Frustration tightened the corners of Fletcher's mouth. ''They're all in their golden years. None of them can handle a three-year-old Labrador retriever who is going to have plenty of energy as soon as he recovers all the way.''

Lily nodded in understanding, even as she forced herself to harden her heart. ''I'm sorry about his owner,'' she said sincerely.

''So is N.L.'' Fletcher knelt down and opened the cage. The Lab struggled to his feet, and clamored out on wobbly legs. Spartacus's tail wagged, then stopped as he caught the wary expression on Lily's face.

"But I can't help you with this, Fletcher," Lily continued firmly as the Lab sat down in front of them and looked up. "But maybe you could take him," Lily suggested as Spartacus continued to gaze at them woefully.

"Can't," Fletcher said, his attitude every bit as stubbornly resistant as her own. "I live in an apartment. This dog needs a house and a yard."

Lily crossed her arms in front of her. Spartacus's well-being aside, she resented the way Fletcher was trying to make this her problem. "Like the one I live in, I suppose," she said dryly.

Fletcher's golden-brown eyes gleamed. "It is big."

"It's huge." And way too much for one person, Lily thought. But the property, which had been in her family for generations, had been entrusted to her, so she couldn't sell it any more than she could get rid of Madsen's Flower Shoppe. But none of that had anything whatsoever to do with what was going on here. "And I still don't buy your excuse for not taking him since there are walking trails that lead to the park that start right across the square." Fletcher could manage if he wanted.

"Only one problem with that," Fletcher shot back while Spartacus sat patiently at their feet, his head moving back and forth like that of a person watching a tennis game. "When I'm not here at the clinic working, I'm out on ranches and farms, taking care of large animals."

"So get Spartacus obedience trained to the highest level by your cousin Susan Hart—" who was famous for her work with search-and-rescue dogs "—and take him literally everywhere you go. You're certainly in a business conducive to it."

Fletcher rejected her suggestion with the same fervor he attached to her desire to date Carson McRue. "A good vet knows better than to get emotionally attached to his patients."

"So, adopt Spartacus and get another vet to take care of him," Lily said.

"N.L. is relying on me to get him well." Fletcher reached down to pet his head, and was rewarded with a single but heartfelt thump of tail. Fletcher straightened and stepped forward slightly, further invading her space. "Besides, there is no room in my life for a dog," he told her, looking deep into her eyes, his smile widening once again. "You, on the other hand, could use the company and protection a big handsome dog like Spartacus offers. He's been through a lot, losing his owner and all. So he's going to need a lot of TLC, especially for the first few weeks."

Lily stepped back a pace, putting a necessary distance between them. "Thereby putting the kibosh on my pursuit of Carson McRue?" she volleyed right back.

Fletcher nodded solemnly. "You know what they say. For all worthwhile endeavors, sacrifices must be made."

Lily rolled her eyes. "You're shameless. You know that?"

Fletcher grinned but didn't deny it as the phone

rang in the other room. Abruptly sobering, he said, "Look, just stay with him for a few minutes, will you?" Fletcher rushed off to answer it.

Spartacus scooted closer. He looked up at Lily with those big sad eyes, silently beseeching her, and wreaking havoc on her tender heart.

"I really have to go," Lily called after him. She was not going to do this. She was not....

Hadn't she promised herself she wouldn't let anyone or anything else tie her down, or distract her from having fun, fun, fun? She did not need to be sitting home baby-sitting a traumatized dog, no matter how lovable.... She needed to be out, fancy-free, kicking up her heels, recovering her lost youth....

"I mean it, Fletcher Hart!" Lily continued.

Fletcher stuck his head back in the room, the still ringing cordless clutched in his hand, his expression reproving. "Really, Lily. What's two minutes petting Spartacus going to cost you?"

"I KNOW WHAT he's doing," Lily told Spartacus as the door shut behind Fletcher, and she heard him start talking on the phone. Unable to help herself, she bent down and gently petted the silky soft back of Spartacus's blond head. "He's trying to get me to bond with you so I'll want to adopt you and take you home with me. That might be a good idea in theory because the old mausoleum I live in could use a little livening up. But the truth is that I'm not sure I still have any love left to give."

Lily swallowed hard around the ache that rose in her throat. "Losing Grandmother Rose was so hard.

I kept thinking I'd feel better.'' But instead she had remained so numb inside. So depressed and alone and hopeless, all at once. Lily stroked him behind the ears, and heard him give a little moan in the back of his throat, not so very different from a cat's purr. But unlike a cat, a species known for its aloofness, Spartacus seemed to want desperately to attach himself to her. And Lily understood that, too. She desperately missed having a family to call her own; the party at Helen Hart's the night before had reminded her of that. ''But then I guess you know a lot about that, too, don't you?'' Lily continued softly, still petting the extremely gentle-natured dog. ''Having lost the only family in your own life.''

''Okay—'' Fletcher burst back in, abruptly all business ''—you can go now.''

The only problem, Lily thought, was that she didn't want to go, since she and Spartacus were just starting to get acquainted.

''I mean it.'' Fletcher shooed her toward the door. ''*Hasta la vista,* baby. Vamoose. See you around.''

Lily straightened with as much dignity as she could manage, wishing she were a lot taller than five foot five inches. She propped both her hands on her hips and demanded indignantly, ''Where did you learn your manners?''

''Didn't,'' Fletcher retorted briskly. ''Can't you tell?''

Lily blew out an exasperated . breath, unsure whether she wanted to kiss him again or kick him in the shin. ''Some things are glaringly apparent.'' To her frustration, he looked pleased—instead of annoyed—by her insult, as if there was nothing he would rather do than work her into a temper and stand there trading insults with her. Spartacus, however, just looked upset to see her leaving. Her heart clenching, despite her efforts to stay emotionally uninvolved, Lily paused at the door. She swallowed hard around the ache in her throat. "Seriously, Fletcher, what is going to happen to N. L. Spartacus?"

The mirth left Fletcher's expression. "I can keep him here another day or so."

Lily's heartbeat sped up another notch. "And then what?" she demanded.

He regarded her steadily. "Like you said, it's really not your problem, Lily."

Silence fell between them, more poignant than ever.

"I'm hoping to find a family for him," Fletcher continued seriously.

"And if you don't?"

He regarded her brusquely. "That's not something you need to worry about."

"Then why did you introduce me to him, bring me over here, have me pet him?" Lily demanded.

Abruptly, the artifice, the teasing fell away. Lily thought she got a glimpse of the real, unguarded man behind his customary mask of cynicism and what-the-hell playfulness. "Because I thought—" A shadow passed over Fletcher's eyes. His expression tightened as he swept a hand through his hair. "It doesn't matter what I thought," he told her in a gruff voice, as Spartacus went back to sit on Fletcher's foot. "I was wrong."

AN HOUR AND A HALF later, Lily discussed the situation with the other bridesmaids as they congregated at a department store in Crabtree Mall in Raleigh, trying on shoes for Janey's wedding. "He's trying to get me to fall in love with N. L. Spartacus."

Janey eyed her. "Seems to be working."

"He thinks if I have a dog I can't continue to try and win my bet with you-all." Lily turned to Susan Hart, Janey's cousin. "Which is why I was thinking…maybe you could take him?" Susan not only operated her own kennels on her farm outside Holly Springs, she headed up the North Carolina Labrador Retriever Rescue Association.

Susan, a voluptuous thirtysomething with champagne blond hair, shook her head wistfully. "I wish I could. But I'm at capacity and then some right now, with dogs that are coming into Labrador Retriever Rescue. You know how it is. Everyone wants their kid to have a puppy at Christmas. Six to nine months later they realize maybe this is too much work after all, and they just take the dog to the pound."

Emma sucked in a breath. "That's terrible."

"I know," Susan agreed. "But a lot of the dogs I get are able to be either adopted out to good homes, or trained to work with police and fire departments around the state. But it takes time to make a placement. Dogs that have been abandoned—like Spartacus—have issues, and require an awful lot of tender loving care, to feel secure again. That's why Fletcher won't take him—he doesn't have the time to give Spartacus the TLC he needs.''

''Or so he says,'' Lily grumbled, wishing Fletcher hadn't made it seem to her like she was N. L. Spartacus's only hope. He had to know—from the way she had let her own needs and desires go unmet when she was taking care of her grandmother—what a soft touch she was. And how very hard it was for her to say no to someone who asked for her help, even when it was for the best. She also wished Spartacus hadn't looked at her with such sad, lonely eyes.

Misunderstanding the depth of her dilemma, Janey murmured, ''You know, you don't have to go through with the bet you made with us on your birthday, Lily. If you didn't we would all understand.''

Lily saw the pity in their eyes. She'd had enough of that, too.

''You really didn't know what you were saying that night,'' Emma continued, gently giving Lily the out they all seemed to feel she needed.

What none of them understood was that the night of her birthday was the first time in years she had felt really and truly vibrantly alive. The only other time was when she'd been arguing with—or kissing—Fletcher, and that was just because he was so darn difficult and made her so hot under the collar.

Lily looked at the young women gathered around her as she tried on a pair of strappy black-and-white sandals. ''So I wasn't just foolish, I was stupid, too? Is that it?''

They all frowned in a way that let her know she

was overreacting. "Reckless, maybe," Hannah conceded, as she put the correct-size shoes back in the box for purchase. "That was quite a loser's penalty you cooked up for yourself."

"One none of us would ever expect you to follow through with," Emma—who had made her own share of life's mistakes—said seriously.

Lily sighed again. They thought she didn't have it in her to be wild and crazy and fear-free. Because of the circumstances she had found herself in back in college, she'd never had the opportunity to embrace her youth the way other coeds did.

But Lily wasn't responsible for anyone else now. It wasn't too late. She could go back, recapture those years, that sense of heady freedom she had always yearned to experience.

"We could even substitute it with something else," Susan Hart suggested brightly. "Like another bar or an event where you buy us all nachos and margaritas."

And didn't that sound dull, Lily thought, even as she absolutely dreaded what lay ahead if she didn't win her bet. "I'm not going to welsh on my wager," Lily said stubbornly, refusing to back down on the audacious claims she had made. As the looks of sympathy around her deepened, she continued with a devil-may-care-air she couldn't begin to really feel. "Besides, it's not as if I'm going to have to do what I swore I would do if I lost. Because I am going to get a date with Carson McRue before this week is up." She just knew it.

Hannah Reid looked worried again. "Has he even spoken to you?"

"No," Lily admitted reluctantly. "But he was eyeing me this morning. And I know that look."

It was the same look that guys always gave her before they worked up the courage to ask her out on a date. It was only later, when they found out how dull, how prim-and-proper she really was at heart, that they lost interest in her. Just as Carson eventually would. But that wasn't the point. The point was to do something daring and unexpected that would expand her horizons, herald a new much more interesting way of life. It was an effort to break completely with the heartache of five years that had been filled with illness and grief, as well as the boredom and depression of the last year. It was a way to recast her as sexy and exciting, instead of sweet and hopelessly angelic.

"What's it to Fletcher anyway who you want to date?" Hannah asked curiously.

Lily shook her head, glad to talk about something other than reconfiguring the bet. Lord only knew. She had been trying to figure out that one herself.

"Could he be jealous?" Janey frowned.

Lily shook her head, protesting, "There's nothing between Fletcher and me."

Susan grinned as she slipped off one pair of sandals and tried on another. "The kiss last night says otherwise."

The heat of embarrassment climbed from Lily's cheeks. "Nothing besides that," Lily amended hastily. "And that kiss didn't mean anything." Even if it felt like it had, at the time....

"Maybe he wishes the kiss did mean something," Emma said sagely.

Lily stiffened her shoulders, trying hard not to remember how movie-star handsome Fletcher had looked standing shoulder to shoulder with Carson McRue in the town square that morning. As if Fletcher were the to-die-for sexy celebrity, and Carson McRue, merely average in comparison. It wasn't as if she had to make a choice between the two of them, anyway. "Don't be ridiculous." She scowled at Emma and the others.

Just because Fletcher looked at her as if he wanted to bed her did not mean he ever would. "Fletcher is just being contrary." Lily continued her argument that nothing was going on between them. "Proving all over again that he is no Sir Galahad. And that romance, or even the hope of it, is for fools."

Silence fell between them. Fletcher had such a reputation as a mischief-loving cynic, no one could dispute that.

Lily looked at Janey. "Why is your brother like that, anyway?"

Janey's lips took on a troubled curve. "I don't know. At some point after our dad died, he just became really cynical and kind of only out for himself, his own ambitions and goals." She paused, shaking her head in bewilderment and regret. "None of us have been able to get close to him emotionally. I mean, I know Fletcher loves us and would—when it came right down to it—do anything for us. But on a day-to-day basis? He's definitely got his own agenda and not a one of us is privy to what that might be."

THE NEXT MORNING, Lily picked up an assortment of fresh doughnuts, four cups of hot coffee and headed over to the barricades. Very little filming had been done the previous day and, judging by the amount of activity going on in front of one of the buildings being used as a backdrop, the cast and crew seemed anxious to make it up.

She had her cover story all prepared—that she was bringing this order by for Carson. But as it turned out, it wasn't necessary to use hijinks for an introduction. The moment Carson McRue laid eyes on Lily, he headed her way, telling the guard standing watch over the barricades to let Lily on through. As she closed the distance between them, he flashed her the cocky grin he used on TV, gallantly took the breakfast she offered and led her toward his trailer.

"I was hoping I'd get the chance to meet you," he told her warmly as someone rushed to open the door for them. "I noticed you yesterday."

He led her inside the incredibly outfitted trailer. It had a living room, a well-equipped kitchen and a bedroom with a king-size bed.

"I wanted to meet you, too, but I couldn't get close to you," Lily said shyly. Although she was momentarily mesmerized by Carson's drop-dead handsomeness, it surprised her that he was just five inches taller than she was and rather slight in build when compared to, say, the six-foot-one, two-hundred-pound, Fletcher Hart.

"I apologize." Ignoring the breakfast she had brought, Carson went to the fridge and got out bottles of imported spring water. "Our producers are a little nuts about the possibility of anyone getting hurt, and with all the cords, power sources and booms—''

"I understand," Lily said with a smile, sitting down on the butter-soft leather sofa. She moved over slightly when he sat down a little too close to her. "It's very responsible of you."

Okay, she was here. This was her dream come true. So why wasn't she more excited? Why didn't she feel the butterflies in her tummy that she felt when she was around Fletcher Hart?

Carson looked her over from head to toe, before returning to laser in on her eyes once again. "So what are you doing tonight?" he asked, drinking deeply.

Cut straight to the chase, why don't you? Lily thought. *But why are you complaining? This will help you win your bet. And you won't have to...* Aware Carson was waiting for her answer, while she was sitting there arguing with herself, Lily said, "I've got a fitting for a bridesmaid dress."

"What about tomorrow night?" he asked, gulping down some more of that designer bottled water.

Lily knew what she would like to be doing—kissing Fletcher Hart again. But since that wasn't about to happen... She shrugged. "I don't have anything planned."

"Perfect, then. It's a date." Carson pursed his lips together thoughtfully. "I'd take you out on the town," he said after a moment, "but we'd be mobbed with my fans."

Lily didn't mind. As long as she accomplished what she had set out to do....

"Tell you what. Why don't you come to my hotel tomorrow evening—the Regency, in Raleigh—and have dinner with me there? Say around nine-thirty?"

Lily was surprised to find she really didn't want to go, at least not as much as she had initially thought she would if she were ever to get herself in this situation. But a bet was a bet and it would serve Fletcher Hart right if she were to win after all he had done to waylay her. "Sounds great," Lily fibbed, still coming to terms with the fact she was about to have dinner with a TV star.

A rap sounded on the trailer door. Carson's young and pretty female assistant stepped in. "Carson? There's a Dr. Fletcher Hart—"

She didn't have a chance to finish as Fletcher shouldered his way in. Fletcher looked at Lily and saw her sitting next to Carson on the leather sofa. He was not pleased.

"How are you doing in finding me a horse to use?" Carson demanded.

"No luck—yet. At least not in the hue you want. But that's not why I'm here. I'm here to collect my woman," Fletcher announced with all the audacity of a big-screen hero.

Lily blinked. And just as audaciously tossed a glance behind, to the left and right of her. Nope. No one else standing there.

Hands braced on his hips, Fletcher regarded Lily with exaggerated patience. "What have I told you about chasing other guys?" he demanded, as unamused by her antics as she was by his.

"Nothing," Lily said, enunciating slowly, as if he

were a dunce. And truly Fletcher was behaving like one.

Fletcher gave Carson a man-to-man glance. "What can I say? This is all a game to her. She likes the chase—" Fletcher reached out, grabbed Lily's hand and tugged her off the sofa "—and I like giving her one." Behaving as if he had some right to be going all possessive on her, Fletcher tucked one muscular arm behind her knees, the other behind her back.

"You can't be serious," Lily groaned, not sure when she had ever felt so shocked and embarrassed, as Carson McRue and his assistant exchanged astonished looks.

Heart racing, she pushed her hands against Fletcher's chest—for all the good it did her. Fletcher swept her off her feet and cradled against his chest. The assistant held the door for him and Fletcher carried Lily down the steps. While everyone looked on with unbridled interest—including the townspeople gathered to watch the action, cast, and crew, directors and producers—Fletcher paused in the middle of the roped-off area. Still holding her cradled in his arms, he slowly, ardently lowered his head to hers.

"Don't. You. Dare," Lily warned.

Chapter Three

But of course Fletcher did, and when the kiss came, it was just as masterful, just as dangerously uninhibited and exciting as before. Lily moaned in a combination of fury and dismay, luxuriating in the feel of his lips on hers. For the first time in her life, she was with a man who wasn't afraid to give her the unrestrained passion she craved, and she reveled in the hard, insistent demand of his mouth on hers, the erotic sweep of his tongue, the way he brought his hands up and tunneled his fingers through her hair.

Lily told herself to resist him. She couldn't let him think he could do this to her again, kiss her just to put on a show, but there was just something about the way he held her and kissed her that totally destroyed her will. He was just so warm and strong and male, so demanding and yet so giving, too. Despite herself, Lily felt herself melt against him. She had never felt so much a woman nor been as aware of any man.

Her nipples were tightening almost painfully beneath her dress. Lower still, there was a definite pressure building, a weakness in her knees. The need, the desire, to take this somewhere quiet, somewhere private, spiraled through her body. But that was crazy, she reminded herself firmly. It wasn't as if she and Fletcher were in love, or could ever be that attached to each other—not with him as deeply cynical and domineering as he was. And she wasn't the kind of woman who would ever react this passionately out of pure physical need, never mind in front of a crowd of onlookers. But with Fletcher Hart holding her against him and kissing her as if she was already his, that was exactly what she was doing.

With effort, Lily pulled herself together and put on the brakes. And it was only then when she had come treacherously close to surrendering to him completely that Fletcher let the tempestuous kiss come to a halt.

Lily told herself she should be furious. But as he released her, heat suffused her and excitement—unlike anything she had ever felt—roared through her. Dimly, she became aware of two things. One, the larger-than-life romance she had been looking for had somehow found her when she least expected it. Not in Beverly Hills or on a private Learjet, but in her hometown of Holly Springs. And two, people were clapping! Hooting and hollering, encouraging Fletcher to take her in his arms and kiss her again. And darned if the son-of-a-gun didn't look tempted.

"You are unbelievable," Lily fumed.

"Yeah, I know." Fletcher tipped the brim of his straw cowboy hat in her direction and grinned at her unrepentantly. "You can thank me later," he promised.

"Thank you?" Lily echoed, all the more incensed.

He leaned close enough to whisper in her ear. "For helping you win your bet."

Lily blinked, and leaned back, fearful that if their bodies touched they would end up kissing again. "What?" Mirroring him, she pretended an insouciance she couldn't begin to feel.

Fletcher acted as if he were imparting top secret information, of the men-only variety. "Men like competition, Lily. I figured if Mr. Magoo—"

"McRue," Lily corrected, noting thankfully that if Carson had witnessed any of what had just gone on, he had since disappeared.

"Whatever," Fletcher continued with a disinterested wave of his hand. "Just that if he saw you kissing me right out in the open like that it might spur him on to try and stake his claim."

Lily glared at Fletcher, wishing she weren't still tingling everywhere he'd touched her...and even more tellingly, everywhere he hadn't. "Is that what you were doing?" she demanded in raging disbelief.

"Yup. Thought it would inspire him to start trying to woo you into accepting a date with him."

Lily blew out an exasperated breath and raked her hands through her hair, trying to restore order to the curls Fletcher had mussed with his fingertips. "Carson McRue does not have to woo me."

Fletcher looked incensed. "Well, he should," he counseled her sternly. "Lily. For heaven's sake! You can't just give it away."

She was going to slug him. She really was. She didn't care who was looking on. Holding on to her temper by a thread, she pushed the words through her teeth. "I am not giving anything away."

Fletcher nodded with mocking approval. "That's good. Play hard to get," he encouraged her baldly. "It works with me."

"And just so you know," Lily continued with a regal toss of her head, "Carson did not need your help getting motivated where I'm concerned. He's already asked me for a date."

For once, Fletcher didn't have a ready comeback. In fact he was silent for so long Lily almost convinced herself he cared whom she went out with.

"When?" Fletcher asked finally in a low, too casual tone.

"Tomorrow evening." Lily smiled at him smugly, glad to see that she at last had the upper hand.

Fletcher seemed to consider that. "Where?"

Lily felt her nerves tighten at the ornery look in his eyes. "None of your business."

Fletcher nodded, looking grim and almost brooding again. "You're right," he said. "It isn't."

That couldn't be disappointment she felt, could it? Lily wondered as silence fell between them once again.

"If you don't care what I do," she reasoned slowly, searching his face for some clue, "then why did you come over here and cut short my conversation with Carson like that?" Why had he carried her off and kissed her like there was no tomorrow. Lily was sure it hadn't been just to create a scene.

Fletcher shrugged his broad shoulders, stuck his hands in the front pockets of his jeans. "Because I thought you might like to say goodbye to N. L. Spartacus,'' he said.

Once again, they were in completely unexpected territory. "Goodbye?" Lily echoed, nonplussed.

Fletcher lifted his left wrist and glanced at his watch. "The guy from the shelter's going to be by anytime now to pick him up." That said, Fletcher turned on his heel and began walking in the direction of the clinic.

"You're kidding." Lily rushed to catch up with Fletcher.

Fletcher said nothing and continued walking, all the way into his clinic. Since office hours weren't set to begin yet, the only person there was his receptionist office manager. She flashed a wan smile, seeming to think the same Lily did about Fletcher's actions.

"I can't believe you are really doing this," Lily said.

Fletcher looked all the more determined as he went through a stack of phone messages the receptionist handed him. "Spartacus needs a home and a family who'll love him. The shelter is his best shot for getting adopted."

"And if he doesn't, then what?" Lily demanded, nearly in tears as she rushed into the room where Spartacus was being kept.

The big yellow lab was lying on his side in the cage, but when he saw them he lifted his head.

His expression turning almost tender it was so compassionate, Fletcher opened the door and motioned the dog out.

Spartacus lumbered slowly to his feet, stretched, then—as if sensing this to-do was all about him—sat abruptly back on his haunches and stared at them stoically, refusing to come out of the cage. And Lily couldn't blame the poor sweet dog, given what Fletcher had in store for him.

"Look—" Fletcher gestured toward Spartacus like a particularly disinterested salesperson "—he's a beautiful animal. Sad but gentle natured."

That, Lily knew, might not save Spartacus from an unwarranted end. "He could get put to sleep!"

Fletcher turned his glance away and didn't respond, reminding Lily that was all part of his job. "Do you want to say goodbye or not?" he demanded harshly, the distant brooding look back in his eyes.

Like clockwork, the shelter guy strode into the reception area, leash in hand. Lily's heart slammed against her ribs and her breath caught in her throat. Numb no longer, she stepped between Spartacus and the two men, stated fiercely, "I am not going to let you do this!"

As if sensing he finally had a savior worth his attentions, Spartacus finally lumbered out of his cage and stood looking up at Lily with his big sad eyes, his tail down between his legs.

Fletcher frowned and folded his arms in front of his chest. He looked ready to square off, too. "You don't have anything to say about it."

"Yes, I do," Lily shot right back, unable to believe how cruel Fletcher was being. Her heart going out to the poor, grieving animal, Lily knelt beside the far-too-skinny yellow lab and wrapped her arms around Spartacus's neck. She regarded Fletcher stubbornly. "I'm taking him home with me."

Fletcher's brows drew together in accusatory fashion. Unwilling to admit she had offered up a solution, he said, "I thought you didn't want a dog."

"I don't," Lily insisted as Spartacus trembled in her arms, his short, dense coat surprisingly soft and silky beneath her hands. He'd had a bath recently, and he smelled of fragrant dog shampoo. "But a lot of people who come into Madsen's Flower Shoppe do. I'll put up a sign. Heck—" she rose gracefully, tilting her head back determinedly, prepared to go toe to toe with Fletcher once again "—I'll take him to work with me and I'll find him a good home with no help at all from you!"

LILY HAD PLENTY of time to regret her actions as she walked the still-somewhat-wobbly-legged N. L. Spartacus across the town square. Her reservations were echoed by her three very talented part-time florists. Mothers all, they juggled family, home and work responsibilities and were grateful for the flexible hours Lily allowed them. "What are you doing with a dog?" Maryellen asked.

"Finding him a home." Briefly, Lily explained, as she got out the digital camera she used for taking photographs of floral arrangements and took a close-up of his handsome face. "The problem is I don't know anything about taking care of a dog."

"Well, don't look at me," the bespectacled Maryellen said as Lily hooked her camera into her computer and printed out the photo while her staff continued to gather round her.

Belinda held up hands made plump by her latest pregnancy. "I've only let the kids get hamsters."

Sheila ran a hand across her perpetually sunburned cheeks. "My expertise is limited to our parakeets."

"Does he even know how to 'stay'?" Maryellen asked as she bent to tentatively pet Spartacus's white-blond head.

Lily had no idea. "I guess I'll find out," she said, getting out what she needed to make up the poster that would find the orphaned pet a new home.

As it happened, she needn't have worried. Spartacus never let her leave his sight. In fact, he was so hypervigilant about where she was and what she was doing, Lily was starting to get a little worried, as she taped a sign in the window of Madsen's Flower Shoppe. It said Wanted—Loving Home For 3-Year-Old Yellow Lab. She had taped a digital photograph of Spartacus beneath it and wrote Ask Inside….

As Lily had hoped, it wasn't long before she had drummed up some interest. A young mother with two elementary-school-age children walked in. They spotted Spartacus sitting tensely beside Lily and headed for him eagerly.

The woman bent down to inspect him. "Is this him?"

Lily smiled. "It sure is."

"What's her name?"

"It's a he. And it's Spartacus." N. L. Spartacus…

The little boy pulled on his mommy's arm. "How come he's not wagging his tail?"

The woman frowned. "He doesn't look very happy. We had in mind something a little more… exuberant."

Lily nodded, understanding the woman's feelings, even as her feelings of protectiveness toward the dog increased tenfold. "He's had a rough time," she stated quietly.

As if on cue, Spartacus moved closer to Lily.

"Well, I wish you luck in finding him a home," the woman said, gathering her kids close and backing toward the door.

The same scenario was repeated throughout the morning. People came in. Spartacus pretty much ignored them all. Even going so far a few times as to turn his head completely away.

"I wonder how hard it is to teach a dog social skills," Maryellen murmured as she put a finished arrangement awaiting pickup into the refrigerator, and then stepped to the front of the shop to check on the progress of the filming on the other side of the square.

"I thought it was kind of automatic for canines to wag their tails and look happy," Belinda said, joining Maryellen at the picture window, her attention also fixated on the TV show scene unfolding before them.

"Me, too," Sheila murmured as the four of them gathered to watch Carson McRue step before the cameras. Someone called "Action!" on a bullhorn and he began conversing with the actor in front of him. The exchange wasn't long. The director nodded his approval. Seconds later, Carson disappeared into his trailer once again.

"Somehow I thought it would be more exciting," Maryellen murmured.

No kidding, Lily thought. She had expected to be riveted when Carson McRue hit town. After all, the handsome, charismatic actor had been a favorite of hers for years. She had watched him turn from a teen heartthrob and player of bit parts into an occasional film actor and the star of his own TV show. But she found he couldn't hold a candle to the other man currently figuring prominently in her life—Fletcher Hart.

And speak of the devil...

Lily turned away from the picture window, hoping he hadn't seen her. "I'll be in the back," she said, beating a hasty retreat to her private office. She had end-of-August bills to be paid, biweekly paychecks to issue.

Spartacus was right beside her.

Seconds later, the bell over the front door rang, and Lily felt as well as heard Fletcher stride in, the atmosphere in her century-old shop changing that much.

"Afternoon, ladies," he said, his deep, low voice supercharging the flower-and-greenery-scented air with his palpable masculinity.

Lily slid sideways in her swivel-based task chair. Able to catch a glimpse of him tipping the brim of his hat toward the three ladies gathered around him, Lily scooted back out of sight and buried her head even deeper in her paperwork.

"Where is she?" Fletcher asked.

One of them must have pointed, because she heard him say, "Thanks." Seconds later, his powerful presence was filling her door frame. As their glances meshed, Lily's heart took a leap, although she couldn't imagine why. It wasn't as if she were letting him or his antics get to her....

Fletcher glanced down at Spartacus, who was sitting beside her. As Fletcher studied Spartacus, the canine surveyed him right back. No words were spoken, no contact made, and yet they seemed to be communicating—rather seriously—with each other just the same. Finally, Fletcher nodded in something akin to grudging approval. "He seems to be doing all right."

For some reason, Fletcher's presumption of incompetence on her part rankled—a lot more than it should have under the circumstances. "Didn't think I could handle him?" Lily challenged sweetly as she tipped back in her chair.

The way he looked at her then, as if he was remembering how it felt to kiss her and wanted to do it again ASAP had her pulse racing. "As you said," he reminded her with a smug male confidence that upped her emotions even more, "you're not a dog person. And that being the case, I figured you might not know what to feed him."

"Dog food?" Lily took a wild guess.

"Actually," Fletcher said seriously, leaning against the edge of her desk to face her, "canned chicken and rice puppy food would be best because it's particularly gentle on the stomach. He really needs to eat small amounts frequently, for the next week or so, while we continue to get his digestive system back in shape.''

The concern in his eyes lessened her annoyance with him. Lily nodded her understanding. ''I'll have to get some.''

''Which is exactly why I'm here,'' Fletcher said. ''It being lunch hour, I figured the three of us could walk down to the pet store and get what you're going to need for him.''

Lily did need a dog-size water dish. The one she was using now was a three-inch plastic flower pot, with a hole in the bottom and a saucer underneath. The one time Spartacus had tried to drink from it, he had knocked it over, gotten startled and hadn't gone near it since.

''Maybe stop in the park on the way back?'' Fletcher continued helpfully.

Lily wasn't very experienced in getting a dog to do what it needed to do in that regard, either. In fact, she hadn't the faintest idea how to go about it. Although she would die before admitting that to Fletcher. ''All right.'' She rose with as much dignity as possible and looked at him sternly. ''But just so we're clear—no more kisses.''

Fletcher grinned and laid a hand across his heart. ''I promise. I'll be every inch the gentlemen where N. L. Spartacus is concerned.''

Lily sighed and rolled her eyes as she got Spartacus's leash and clumsily attached it to his collar. ''You know what I mean, Dr. Hart.''

Fletcher's eyes sparkled all the more. ''Indeed I do.''

"I HEAR YOU AND FLETCHER had lunch in the park today," Janey said when Lily arrived at the bridal shop for the final fitting of her bridesmaid dress.

"Word gets around," Lily surmised happily.

Janey shot her a knowing glance. "What do you expect when you're seen kissing him in the town square at eight in the morning, in front of a crowd of oh, say, a couple hundred of the most talkative citizens in town?"

Lily tried—and failed—to erase that romantic interlude from memory. Pretending it had meant nothing to her, she waved a hand disparagingly. "Fletcher was just fooling around."

"Knowing my brother the way I do, that's obvious." Janey paused, her concern deepening as she handed Lily the dress she was to try on for the seamstress. "What's your excuse?"

Lily swallowed as she slipped out of the sundress she had worn to work. That was the problem. She had no excuse for her increasingly potent reaction to Janey's brother. All she had to do was be near Fletcher or see him and her heart speeded up, her knees went weak and every resistance seemed to fade. "He caught me off guard. And he was just doing it to help me win my bet."

Janey helped Lily slip into the sophisticated black-and-white bridesmaid dress. "You're kidding."

Lily shrugged. "That's what Fletcher claims."

"Hmm." Janey looked unconvinced as Lily stepped up onto the dressmaker's stool to look at herself in the three-way mirror. "Well, that's a new one, anyway."

Lily turned this way and that and found the alterations had been flawless. The long column dress fit her like a second skin. "Why? Has Fletcher done this before? Gotten between a woman and her potential beau just for sport?"

"No. Actually, he hasn't." Janey looked seriously worried once again. "Usually it's women pursuing him."

Satisfied, Lily stepped off the stool and turned so Janey could unzip her. "Do they ever catch him?" Fletcher more often dated women outside of Holly Springs. Probably to avoid the local gossips knowing more than he wanted them to know.

Janey sighed dispiritedly as she helped Lily out of the satin gown. "If they do, it's not for long. Which is why I want you to be careful. He's my brother and I love him dearly, but I wouldn't wish a gotta-have-my-space guy like him on my worst enemy. So be careful."

"Believe me," Lily fibbed, as she changed back into her sundress, "I am in no danger of losing my heart to him. The only reason I was with Fletcher at noon was because I needed help getting some basic supplies for Spartacus."

Janey studied her contemplatively. "And Fletcher helped you pick them out?"

"As well as paid for them," Lily said, feeling both pleased and puzzled about that. For a guy who had been trying to send the homeless dog to the pound only hours earlier, Fletcher had been very generous, purchasing all the dog necessities as well as several toys and a book on dog basics. Then he arranged the pet store to deliver all the supplies to her home that evening at five, so she could put them all away. ''The only reason he bought me lunch was that we were both in the park with Spartacus, and we had corn dogs and sodas. It was no big deal. Believe me.''

Janey looked even more skeptical but wisely changed the subject. ''So what have you got on your agenda this evening?'' she asked as the seamstress zipped up Lily's now perfectly fitting dress and got it ready to go.

''I'm going into Raleigh to do some shopping,'' Lily declared, pushing the lingering image of Dr. Fletcher Hart from her mind. She had a date with Carson McRue the following evening. And she was determined it would not only help her win the first part of her bet with her friends, but also mark a turning point for her. Somehow, some way, she wanted it to be a stepping stone out of her previously humdrum, sheltered existence, and change her life forever.

FLETCHER HAD HOPED to see Lily when he went to pick up his tuxedo at the formalwear shop that evening—since the fitting for the bridesmaid dresses was going on at the same time—but found out she had already left.

Doing his best to quell his disappointment, he tried everything on and headed out with formal clothes in tow. Returning home, he tried to eat some dinner and settle in with the endless paperwork that came with running the vet clinic, but again and again his thoughts turned to the blond-haired, blue-eyed angel who had very quickly come to dominate his life in recent days.

And that presence had to do with a lot more than the promise he had made to her grandmother Rose. It had to do with Lily.

He had started out just trying to divert her. All he'd wanted was to keep her from making a fool of herself over Carson McRue and to prevent Lily from getting permanently hurt in the bargain. And somehow in the midst of all that, he had ended up kissing her—twice—and wanting to make her his own.

Which in a sense made him just as bad as the Hollywood actor, because Fletcher had no intention of ever getting married or spending his life trying to make any one woman happy for the rest of their days. And that was exactly what a woman like Lily Madsen deserved—a man who could and would give her all that and more.

Which meant he had to go back to trying to waylay Lily from hooking up with Carson, while at the same time maintaining a more gentlemanly demeanor himself. Not an easy task, especially for someone who was as prone to screw-ups as he was when it came to those he cared about.

He was still figuring out how to achieve such an impossible feat when the phone rang at ten o'clock. He saw on the caller ID that it was Lily and picked up immediately.

"Hey, Lily, what's up?" he said as casually as if

he hadn't been sitting around thinking about her all evening, wishing he were a better man so he could pursue her all-out—not just for now, but for keeps. Wishing he hadn't made that promise to her grandmother Rose to protect her and keep her from harm's way and any and all undeserving males. Just like him.

"Oh, Fletcher." Lily's voice caught on a heartfelt sob that went straight to Fletcher's gut.

Heart pounding, Fletcher vaulted out of his chair.

"I don't know what happened! I just left Spartacus for a short while. But he can't even stand up now and he's—he's b-bleeding!"

"Hang on, Lily," Fletcher said, reaching for his vet bag. "I'll be right there."

Chapter Four

Lily met Fletcher at the front door of the stately white Victorian, with pine-green trim, that she had inherited after her grandmother Rose's death. Although she was trying desperately to pull herself together, it was clear she had been crying. "Where is he?" Fletcher asked, all business.

Lily's lower lip trembled as she replied, "In the laundry room, where I had him while I was gone."

Together, they hurried through huge, high-ceilinged rooms filled with expensive antiques and dark heavy velvet draperies Fletcher guessed were nearly as old as the house. Lily had turned on lamps here and there, but none was enough to illuminate the majestic hallway that ran the length of the house.

She dashed through an equally out-of-date kitchen, where take-out bags from a popular Italian eatery still sat on the heavy oak table, past an open-shelf pantry into a room that had been converted to handle a modern washer and dryer. A drying rack, filled with all sorts of sheer and lacey unmentionables stood in one corner. Spartacus was curled up against the opposite wall, his back to the cushioned bed Lily had laid out for him. Blotches of dried blood dotted the white and black linoleum floor. Spartacus had been licking his front paws rapidly when they entered, but stopped and regarded them anxiously.

Fletcher got down on his haunches. "Where is he bleeding?" he asked, already starting to examine him.

Lily teared up again as she knelt down in front of Spartacus. "Right here. On the bottom of his paws."

She tried to show Fletcher, but Spartacus pulled his legs back and hid his paws beneath his torso so they couldn't get at them.

Fletcher moved in closer—his leg inadvertently touching hers in the process—and gently but firmly guided Spartacus over onto his side. Spartacus looked up at him with big sad eyes, but didn't struggle as Fletcher carefully examined the wet, saliva-stained paws. The skin between the digits was swollen and inflamed, painful to the slightest touch, and bleeding in spots. "I don't see anything stuck in here, like a piece of glass or a thorn or anything," Fletcher said, stroking Spartacus with one hand while continuing to examine him with the other.

"Then why was he chewing on them like that?" Lily demanded, petting Spartacus, too.

Fletcher looked into Spartacus's handsome face, continuing to reassure the big lab, even as he spoke. "Fear. Anxiety. He was probably scared, being left alone, and attempted to comfort himself—the same way a baby sucks on his or her thumb. And got a little carried away."

Lily sat back on her haunches, the skirt of her

sundress riding up over her thighs. "Well, what can we do?" she asked, looking eager to help.

Ignoring the pressure building in his groin, the way it always did when he was near her like this, Fletcher rummaged through his brown leather vet bag. "I've got some Gentamicin sulfate spray that will help. We can put it on three times a day until his paws are better."

Lily raked her teeth across the softness of her lower lip as she turned troubled eyes to him. "Won't he lick it off?"

"Yes, he will," Fletcher replied, aware this was the first time he had ever seen Lily with her guard completely down. Even at her grandmother Rose's funeral, she had kept some of those prim-and-proper barriers around her heart, allowing people to only get so close, never reaching out to anyone. It had almost been as if she'd felt she would have been breaking some code of proper Southern womanhood by letting herself be vulnerable to anyone. At the time he had understood—he, too, liked keeping his guard up, never more so than when he was hurting. It was somehow easier that way. Now, he wondered if they both hadn't made a mistake....

Aware Lily was waiting for him to continue instructing her on the application of the medicine, Fletcher said, "Which is why it's a good idea to distract him with a walk or something right after you apply the spray."

Lily nodded, understanding, yet still looking a little apprehensive. She swallowed. "When he got up before, he was limping. That's how he got blood all over the floor.''

Fletcher nodded thoughtfully. He smiled at Lily, noting the redness around her eyes was subsiding. ''Got any old cotton socks you don't need anymore that you wouldn't mind donating to Spartacus here?''

''Sure.'' Lily was already scrambling to her feet, with another tempting flash of silken thigh. ''I'll go get them.''

While Lily ran off, Fletcher turned his attention to the rack of unmentionables flying like a sexy flag over his head. He knew he shouldn't be looking, but what the hell, it was probably the only chance he would ever have to discover what kind of lingerie Lily Madsen favored. From the looks of it—skimpy. Those were thongs, not grandma panties. And sheer low-cut bras of a size that looked…exactly right. Not too big, not too small.

Lily bustled back in. Catching the direction of his glance, she blushed all the harder. ''A gentleman wouldn't have looked,'' she scolded him primly.

Fletcher grinned. He didn't know why but he sure enjoyed getting under her skin. ''I think we've already established I'm no gentleman.''

Her lips formed a skeptical pout. ''You won't get an argument there.''

She knelt beside him in a drift of lilac perfume, offering up a dozen or so socks in a rainbow of colors. ''These okay?'' she asked.

''Perfect,'' Fletcher said, thinking Spartacus was going to be the best-dressed Lab around. Now for the hard part. Frowning, he predicted, ''Spartacus is probably not going to like this. So I want you to get around behind him, so you can cradle his head in your lap and comfort him while I work.'' Fletcher got a roll of surgical tape and scissors from his bag and set them down beside the antiseptic wash and aforementioned antibiotic-analgesic-anti-inflammatory spray.

''Just talk to him, sweetheart,'' Fletcher instructed Lily, as she scooted around to comply with Fletcher's instructions.

''Did you hear that?'' Lily asked as she cuddled and petted Spartacus as if she'd had the sad-eyed yellow Lab since birth instead of for just one day. ''He just called me sweetheart.'' She frowned at Fletcher, the prettiest picture of reproof he had ever seen. ''No one calls me sweetheart,'' Lily continued sternly.

Fletcher did his best to stifle a grin. ''Maybe they should,'' he murmured right back.

Lily drew an indignant breath. ''I beg your pardon!''

''Well—'' Fletcher shrugged, relishing the fact he was getting under her skin once again ''—it never hurts to loosen up.''

Leave it to Fletcher Hart, Lily thought, to get straight to the heart of the matter. Loosen up was exactly what she had been trying to do the night of her twenty-fifth birthday party, and every day before and since. Loosening up was what had gotten her in such trouble. Because of that, she was either about to be embarrassed by losing a bet she never should have made—or in a situation with an actor who, in reality, might be a whole lot different than the fun and affable character he portrayed on TV.

"Just keep petting and stroking," Fletcher instructed as he shook the bottle, gently separated the digits on Spartacus's paw, applied a topical cleanser and then sprayed it liberally with the medication. "Yeah, I know, buddy," Fletcher soothed when Spartacus yelped and struggled to be free. He held him down flat with the palms of his hands. "That last stuff stings. But the medicine is going to help, you'll see."

Fletcher continued soothing Spartacus as he worked on his paws, first cleaning, then medicating them with spray and finally pulling on socks and securing them in place with white surgical tape. By the time Fletcher had finished, Spartacus was looking up at Fletcher with a mixture of trust and affection.

"You're really good with him," Lily noted.

Fletcher shrugged. "It's my job." He dropped the scissors back in his veterinary bag and handed the roll of tape and spray to her. "Keep these. You'll need 'em when it comes time to apply the medicine again."

Lily blinked. "You don't expect me to do this by myself!"

"That's usually the procedure."

Lily looked doubtfully at Spartacus. He really had not liked that spray, but had also been smart enough to realize he was outnumbered. If she were to attempt it solo, there was no guaranteeing he would be anywhere near as cooperative. And she didn't want to screw up by accidentally spraying Spartacus in the eye or something. "Well, couldn't you come by to help me with this tomorrow before you go to work?"

"Lily Madsen!" Fletcher scolded her playfully before giving her a heated once-over. "Are you inviting me for breakfast?"

Lily continued petting Spartacus and tried not to think how debonairly sexy Fletcher looked whenever he was teasing her. "Is it required?"

He favored her with a flirtatious smile that did funny things to her insides as he got lithely to his feet. "For a free house call that time of day?" He nodded with mock solemnity. "I should think so."

Lily wrinkled her nose at him, trying not to think how intimate it would feel to start her day off with him by her side. "I hope you're not expecting a four-course meal," she said.

Fletcher looked at her gently. "A cup of coffee and bagel would be fine."

Lily tried not to think how much she enjoyed having Fletcher around. "All right. What time?"

Fletcher shrugged his broad shoulders, then held out a hand and assisted her to her feet, his fingers lingering warmly over hers. "Seven?"

Lily groaned as she gently disengaged their hands. Not sure where this would lead, or where she wanted it to lead. "I'm not that much of a morning person," she said.

He picked up his vet bag, all lazy swaggering male. "Seven-thirty?"

"Fine," she nodded. "In the meantime, what am I going to do with him?" Lily pointed at Spartacus, who was already investigating the tape holding up his socks, nosing and licking it.

"Where were you planning to have him sleep tonight?"

"Right here, in the laundry room."

"Obviously, that is not going to work."

Recalling what had happened the last time Spartacus had been closeted up there alone, Lily sighed. "No foolin', Dr. Fletcher Hart. Where would you suggest?"

"In your bedroom. At least for now. Just put the cushion up there and then he can curl up where he can see you. Dogs are pack animals. They want to be part of the pack. And right now, like it or not, you're his pack."

"So are you."

Fletcher's eyes lit up. "If that's an invitation—"

Lily blushed and replied hastily, "No!"

Fletcher grinned again, as if thinking about all the ways he might get her to change her mind on that, then sobered, and returned—with surprising seriousness—to the subject at hand. "I assume you weren't planning to go up to bed right away?"

Only, Lily thought, if I were going up there with you.

Then wondering where that thought had come from, she pushed the idea of making hot, wild, wonderful love to Fletcher as far from her mind as possible. Clearing her throat, she attempted to be as serious as he was being. "I thought I might eat my dinner first, before I turn in. And Spartacus needs to be fed one more time, too," she said, having taken

Fletcher's advice to feed Spartacus small meals frequently until his stomach was back to normal again. A fact that seemed to please Spartacus no end.

Ignoring the sexual tension simmering between them, Lily got out a can of dog food and tossed it his way. Fletcher made a one-handed catch, then caught the can opener, too. "You want to stay and eat?" Lily asked.

"Dog food?" Fletcher furrowed his brow in comical fashion. "I don't think so."

"I meant takeout," Lily explained. "I'll even share with you, if you want. As payment for this house call."

His eyes glimmered. She knew what he was thinking, even if he didn't come out and say it. "It's the only payment you're going to get, Fletcher," she warned with simpering Southern belle sweetness, "unless you'd like some flowers."

He looked over her shoulder as she opened up the take-out bags from a popular Italian restaurant. "What is it?"

Lily opened her oven and slid the foil container in to reheat. "Chicken cannelloni, salad and bread sticks."

His brow lifted enthusiastically. "And dessert?"

Lily nodded deeply in acknowledgment. "Tiramisu, of course."

His grin broadened. "You've just made an offer I can't refuse."

He knelt and spooned food into a bowl for Spartacus. Unhappy with the socks on his legs, Spartacus tried to stand, then decided against it. He made do by scooting forward to the bowl and eating while lying on his stomach. Watching, Lily predicted, "He's going to get a crick in his neck."

"Probably."

More silence. Lily was suddenly a little nervous. First-date nervous. Not that this was a date…

Gulping, she fought the anxiety starting up inside her. The feeling that said she wasn't nearly woman enough for a man like Fletcher Hart—never mind as experienced as he was probably used to….

She turned away from the mixture of pleasure and expectation radiating in his golden-brown eyes. "I'd offer you a glass of wine but the only liquor we have in the house is a bottle of crème de menthe that is about oh…six years old. So…?" She left the question hanging.

He shook his head. "Thanks, anyway. I'll pass."

As their glances meshed and held all Lily could think about was kissing him again. Not that she had any business doing that, either. She might be looking for adventure, she wasn't looking for a broken heart. Fletcher was a man who could definitely stomp her romantic soul to pieces. All it would take was a little lovemaking, followed by a lot of his trademark aloofness and cynicism.

"You really should have a dog, you know," Lily said as she got out a couple of plates and glasses.

Fletcher lounged against the counter, arms folded in front of him, ankles crossed. He knit his brows together and teased in a soft, low voice that sent thrills coursing over her body, "Isn't that what I said to you?"

Being careful not to get too close to him, lest she lose her focus, Lily continued setting the table. "I mean it. You're so gentle with animals."

He shrugged, continuing to make himself at home. "My job to be."

"He'd make a great companion." Lily continued her sales pitch enthusiastically.

The brooding look was back in Fletcher's eyes. "What?" she said.

He studied her, as if trying to decide how much he wanted to tell her about what he was thinking and feeling. Finally, he released a short unhappy breath and said casually, "It's not something I usually discuss, but…I—we—had a dog once. When I was a kid."

"Really? What kind?"

This was a surprise. Lily couldn't recall the Harts having any pets when they moved back to Holly Springs, after Fletcher's dad died. Helen Hart had been too busy caring for her brood of six kids and turning the family home she had inherited into the premiere wedding facility in the Carolinas, the Wedding Inn.

"A beagle. Lucky didn't mind very well and I wasn't very good at taking care of him."

Lily tensed, able to see his dog had come to a bad end. "How old were you?" she asked softly, edging nearer.

The deeply cynical look was back in Fletcher's eyes. "Eight when I got him, ten when he got hit by a car and died."

"Oh, Fletcher." Lily reached out and touched his arm.

"It was my fault." Lips pressed together grimly, he continued in a low, self-deprecating voice. "I was taking him on a walk and he was pulling every which way. I got tired of being dragged around. So I just unsnapped the leash and let him go where he wanted. Which was basically everywhere," Fletcher admitted, shaking his head, his guilt over that apparent. "Into neighbors' flower gardens and on their porches, and eventually right out into the street where he got hit by a car driving by."

Her heart went out to him as she saw the sadness radiated in his eyes. She had lost her own cat to old age, having known the end was coming. She could only imagine how a senseless death like this must have hurt—especially for a child.

"I remember the screech of the brakes as the driver tried to stop, that awful thud, when you knew, even before you saw…. Then just standing there, frozen, unable to believe it had really happened. Then Lucky let out another high-pitched yelp and I rushed over to help him."

Looking angry and upset with himself, Fletcher continued telling her what had happened to his pet. "He was bleeding pretty bad and in a lot of pain. I comforted him as best I could but he died in my arms before the car's driver and I could even get him in the car to take him to the animal hospital up the street." Moisture glistened in his eyes.

Lily studied the tortured expression on Fletcher's face. It was clear he had never gotten over the loss or forgiven himself for his part in the accident. "Is that what prompted you to become a vet?" Lily asked gently.

He nodded. "I wanted to know what to do. I wanted to be able to save him." He paused and ran a hand over his face. "Of course, now I know that even a vet couldn't have done anything for Lucky. His injuries were just too severe."

"And you never had another dog."

"Nope. Losing one was enough."

Lily understood that, too. After Penelope had died she hadn't wanted another cat, either, although there were a lot of people who felt she should have run right out and adopted another Persian, just like the cat she had lost. At the time it had been unthinkable. Now that she had another pet in her life, albeit temporarily, she was beginning to wonder if her friends hadn't been right.

Fletcher turned his glance away from her. It landed on the shelf with the dark green liqueur bottle. "You know, on second thought, I think I'll take you up on that crème de menthe," he said as he pulled it off the decorative shelf to the right of the kitchen sink. He handed it to her, his fingers brushing hers in the process. "Put a little milk in it, would you?"

Lily knew what he was doing—distracting them. Willing to give him the emotional room he needed, she made a face before blowing the dust off the bottle and pouring a fingerful into a juice glass. "Somehow, I never imagined you drinking this," she murmured as she added milk and ice and gave it a stir.

Fletcher put the glass to his lips and took a sip of

the minty pale green liquid, grimacing only slightly as it went down. "Oh, there's lots you don't know about me," he teased.

Their eyes met again. "I'm beginning to realize that, too," Lily said, realizing she hadn't felt this much in ages. Maybe…ever.

"WELL, THAT WAS pretty darn good for warmed-up takeout," Fletcher said half an hour later as he pushed his plate away.

"I thought so, too." Lily smiled. Between the two of them, they had eaten every bite while they talked about the upcoming wedding they were both participating in, as well as other wedding parties they had been in.

"So now what?" Fletcher asked as he got up to help her clear the table.

Finished with his own meal, Spartacus curled up beside his food dish and began working diligently on the tape that secured the sock-bandages in place.

Lily glanced up at the clock on the kitchen wall. It was almost midnight. Where had the time gone? "I've got to get him upstairs. You think he'll walk?"

"Um—" Fletcher ran his fingers through the shaggy layers of his honey-brown hair "—just a suggestion, but I think you might want to take Spartacus out back to do whatever he needs to do before he turns in for the night. Unless of course you want to be awakened by urgent whining at 3:00 a.m.?"

Something about the roguishness of his expression brought out the mischievous side of her. "His or yours?'' Lily asked with a straight face and was rewarded with a full-bellied laugh from Fletcher.

"Why, Miss Madsen." He looked her up and down in a comical parody of shock. "I do believe you just made an off-color remark."

A shock, Lily knew, since she had the reputation for being one of the primmest and most proper young women in all of Holly Springs. "Must be the company I'm in," she quipped. "As I never talk that way." Grandmother Rose would not have allowed it.

"A pity." He teased her with a look as he clasped her elbow and chivalrously led her in the direction he wanted her to go. "I rather like the newfound devilish side of you."

It took some coaxing but they finally got Spartacus to stand up. He didn't seem convinced he could walk at first, but with a little more coaxing and some nuggets of dog treat that Fletcher just happened to have in his pants pocket, Spartacus discovered he could walk with socks on his paws. He didn't have much traction on the polished wood floors, but once he hit the grass outside, he was doing just fine.

Lily and Fletcher stood in the darkness of the backyard. Once again, all she could think about was kissing him—and not for show or some other cockeyed purpose this time, but because she just wanted to feel his lips on hers once again, so sure and warm and male.

But he didn't make a move.

And soon Spartacus had done what was necessary.

"Want some help taking that dog bed and Spartacus upstairs?'' Fletcher asked casually as they headed back inside.

Why not delay his inevitable departure, Lily thought. She had never had so much fun with a man—not even on a real date—as she had with Fletcher in the past two days. ''Sure,'' Lily said. Although it would mean having Fletcher in her bedroom…a dangerous proposition indeed, if not for their trusty canine chaperone.

Lily led the way upstairs. Fletcher followed, the dog cushion in his arms. Spartacus was right behind him.

They walked down the long dimly lit hall, past her grandmother's room with its big four-poster canopy bed, to the pink-and-white room Lily'd had since she was a child. There was a canopy bed in there, too, but it was a single, sized for a child. She had never thought about it much. Never thought about switching bedrooms. Until she saw the look on Fletcher's face.

No wonder she was having trouble growing up, Lily realized with sudden shock. She might run a business in her professional life, but at home and in her private time, she hadn't made any strides at all. She was stuck in a holding pattern she wanted very much to break out of.

''Where should I put this?'' Fletcher said, kind enough not to mention the juvenile decor.

Aware of the embarrassed color moving from her throat into her face, Lily tried hard to concentrate on the problem at hand, instead of what an experienced man like Fletcher must think of her. "Where do you think it should go?" she asked a little stiffly.

"Probably in the corner," Fletcher set the dog bed down next to the window seat that overlooked the front yard. "So he'll feel protected, but can still see you."

"Thank you." Lily smiled the brisk professional smile she reserved for customers at the shop, then, still feeling self-conscious as all-get-out, led the way back downstairs. Fletcher followed her, but Spartacus, obviously deciding it was too much trouble to go all the way down again, remained at the head of the stairs with his chin resting on the hall floor and his paws hanging over the edge.

Again, Fletcher lingered, as if he didn't want to go any more than she wanted him to leave. "Maybe I should write down all my numbers for you," he said finally, his tone as crisp and businesslike as hers had become. "So if you have any more problems, you'll be able to reach me."

Lily nodded. Did he want to kiss her as much as she wanted to kiss him? "Good idea," she said.

Fletcher looked casually at home once again. "Got a paper and pen?"

Lily nodded. "In the study, by the phone." Again, she led the way, switching on lamps as she went. Like everything else in the big old house, the furnishings were covered with old-fashioned lace doilies and slip-covered in faded floral prints.

Without really looking at the notepad she picked up, Lily handed it to him, as well as a pen.

Fletcher started to turn the page, then stopped and flipped it back.

He stared at the writing, a bemused expression on his face. "What in the name of all that's sweet and innocent is this?" he asked.

Chapter Five

Lily flushed, looking—in Fletcher's estimation—even prettier and more delectably sexy than she had when he arrived to help her with Spartacus. "Just never you mind," she said heatedly, reaching for the notepad.

Fletcher knew he should just give her "list" back, but having already seen as much as he had, the temptation was too great to ignore. "'Things I Want Before I'm Twenty-Six,'" he read out loud, surprised but pleased to have this unexpected window into Lily's soul. "'One. Stay up all night with a guy, having the best time of my life.'"

He paused and looked over at her, trying not to fantasize about what it would be like to personally help her fulfill that dream. "That doesn't sound so hard," Fletcher drawled lazily, to cover the fast growing ache inside him. "Provided, of course, you're with the right man."

Lily squared her shoulders and aimed a killer look at him. "I'm so glad you approve."

Grinning, Fletcher returned his attention to the list.

"'Two,'" he read. "'Receive flowers.'" Then he quirked a brow at her, wondering what that meant.

"No one ever sends a florist flowers," Lily explained, not bothering to hide her disappointment about that.

He moved closer, liking the way her pale blond curls shimmered in the light of the study. "What do you usually get?"

She shrugged and perched on the arm of a faded, floral-upholstered club chair. Swinging one trim ankle back and forth, she tossed her head and announced, "I don't usually get presents from men."

"Well, now, that's a shame," Fletcher said. He liked the droll humor in her voice and the exasperated color flowing into her cheeks.

"You can stop reading now." She stretched across him to get her list, the softness of her breasts brushing his forearm.

"I don't think so." He whisked the paper out of her reach, stepped back and read, "'Three. Not be afraid to speak up for myself or do what I want to do, regardless of what anyone else thinks.'" He frowned, wondering what kind of questionable activity she had in mind. And if that activity concerned one Hollywood actor.

Lily glared at him from beneath her thick blond lashes. "It's not up to you to approve or disapprove of my goals, Fletcher Hart," she said.

Maybe not. But given that promise he had secretly made to her grandmother Rose, Fletcher decided he was doing so just the same. To that end, he was going to have to keep a closer eye on Lily, at least while Carson McRue was in town.

Fletcher continued going over the items on the list. "'Four. Choose my own career.'"

Huh? He lifted his eyes to hers.

Lily lifted her delicate hands, palm up. "Madsen's Flower Shoppe was just handed to me. I never said I wanted to be a florist. Ditto this house. I never said I wanted it, either. It was just given to me."

"So sell the business," Fletcher advised, a tad impatiently.

Lily blinked. "And not the house?"

Fletcher cast a look around, taking in the sturdy-built and spacious, high-ceilinged rooms. Lily could rear half a dozen kids here and not feel the least bit crowded. "It's a great place. Or it would be," Fletcher allowed, meeting her eyes again, "if you made it your own. I think you might want to hang on to it and try that before you ditch it altogether."

"Hmm. I guess I really hadn't thought about that," Lily murmured, looking perplexed.

"'Five.'" Fletcher continued down her list of things she wanted to achieve before the next birthday rolled around. "'Be swept off my feet.'" He looked at her and, unable to resist, teased, "Didn't I just do that today at the town square?"

"So cross it off my list," Lily said dryly.

"Love to," Fletcher quipped right back as his gaze focused on the next important item on her To Do list, the one that had caught his attention in the first place. "'Six—be loved in that special man-woman way.'"

Lily was blushing fire-engine red now.

Fletcher put the paper back down momentarily, feeling more like her grandmother-appointed chaperone than he preferred. "You want to explain that?" he demanded sternly.

"No. As a matter of fact, I do not," Lily replied just as stonily.

Good, Fletcher thought, because that meant she wasn't quite as ready to accomplish that particular feat as she wanted to be. He picked up the list again. "And last but not least, 'Number seven. Access my inner bad girl or be as sexy as I know I can be.'" He blinked, and read it again just to be sure. That was what it said, all right. "Whoa! Miss Lily!" he chided.

Lily wrinkled her nose at him. "Don't pretend to be shocked." She gave him a pouty look that dared him to haul her into his arms and kiss her again. With even less reserve than before... Fortunately, for both of them his conscience intervened. "But I am shocked," he told her. More to the point, he was worried. Given the nature of Lily's To Do list, Carson McRue was definitely the wrong man for Lily to be hanging around, even for a short time.

Lily reached for her "list" again. This time, he let her take it from him.

Fletcher thought about Lily's naiveté and the promise he had made, and knew he couldn't just forget what he had just learned. Or what it was she was about to do.

"You can go now," Lily said, taking his elbow.

Like hell, Fletcher thought, as he resisted her attempt to push him toward the door. Instead, he took the notepad from her, and turned the page and wrote down all his numbers for her. "If it's during the day," he told her seriously, "try the office first—they always know where I am. If it's after hours, and I don't answer my office or home phones, call my cell. But I don't answer my cell unless I'm out and about. Otherwise I keep it off. Okay?"

Lily ran her fingers through her hair impatiently. "I'm not going to need you," she stated stubbornly.

Like heck she didn't, Fletcher thought, as he left the notepad on her desk. Lily Madsen needed him more than she could say.

"Well, just in case," Fletcher reiterated firmly, "you'll know how to find me." It was high time he got out of there, before he gave in to impulse, took her in his arms and did something terribly reckless to fulfill at least a few of the items on her "list." Something they'd both likely regret.

"ARE YOU SURE you want to do this?" Hannah Reid asked Lily the following evening, when she came over to "pet-sit" Spartacus and hopefully prevent another canine-anxiety attack.

No, as a matter of fact, Lily was no longer sure she wanted to go on a date with Carson McRue. Part of it was nerves, of course—she had never been on a date with anyone famous and worried about hopelessly embarrassing herself. And the other part was her reluctance to have her idealistic image of the handsome TV star crushed. She had admired Carson McRue, Hollywood P.I., from afar for so long. She'd let him dominate her wishful thinking when it came to romance, never dreaming she would ever get to see him in person, never mind go on a date with him. And there had been comfort in that, in a weird way. Maybe because her romantic notions of the perfect moment with the perfect man were within her control in a way real life was not.

In her daydreams, people didn't get cancer or die—or say or do the wrong things. It her daydreams, everything could be perfect and scripted and happily ever after without risk. Real life, on the other hand, carried the threat of the heartache Dr. Fletcher Hart was certain she was going to endure. But she wouldn't think about that now. Wouldn't let Fletcher ruin her daydream come true.

"It's half the bet," Lily said, to her friend. If she dined with Carson tonight, then all she would have left to do was somehow wangle a ride on his private jet when he left North Carolina at the end of the week. And the residents of Holly Springs would see her in a whole new way. No longer someone to be pitied, for the familial losses and tragedies she had endured. But as a gusty and hopefully sexy woman who wasn't afraid to pursue what she wanted in this life, someone who had actually been on a date—and a private jet—with a dashing TV star.

Hannah looked at the outfit Lily had selected for the date. She didn't have to say anything. Lily knew it was quite unlike her. Which was, of course, the point. "You've got nothing to prove," Hannah said.

"Yes, I do," Lily said soberly. "I've been in a

rut, Hannah.'' My entire life, it seems. Especially, lately.

Hannah waved off further explanation. "You don't have to tell me. I inherited a family business and a house, too.''

"But—?'' Lily prodded, realizing that Hannah Reid was dissatisfied with her life, too. And that surprised her. Lily had always imagined the perennial tomboy, who even now was clad in baggy engineer-stripe overalls, a form-fitting black T-shirt and scuffed running shoes, was content just hanging out and being "one of the guys.''

Hannah released her long, wavy auburn hair from its ponytail. "People around here see me as a grease monkey, who only cares about fixing up or maintaining classic cars. As a result, life gets pretty darn dull. I've been thinking about ways to break free of all that, and become someone else entirely, too. At least for part of the time. But I'm not sure I want the whole town watching when I do.''

Lily tried to make sense of that but couldn't. "What are you talking about?''

"Well—'' Hannah took a brush out of her canvas carryall and ran it through her hair "—you've heard about people who go on vacation and sort of become someone or something else while they live it up, and then go back to their normal lives...and reality.''

"And my date tonight with Carson is not...reality.'' Lily guessed where this was going.

"The fact you and Carson McRue are from two different worlds is probably what you find so attractive,'' Hannah continued thoughtfully.

No, Lily thought. *Attractive* was Fletcher Hart. It was just too bad, due to his cynical, never-stay-with-any-one-woman-for-long attitude that nothing of substance would ever develop there.

LILY'S NERVES HAD CALMED marginally when she arrived at the five-star Raleigh hotel where Carson McRue was staying. She handed her car over to valet parking and walked into the lobby, heading straight for the concierge desk as directed and identified herself to the elegantly dressed man. "Hi. I'm Lily Madsen."

"Oh, Miss Madsen! We've been expecting you!"

So this was the star treatment.

The concierge handed her a small parchment envelope containing an electronic hotel key.

"I need a key to get into a private dining room?" Lily asked.

The man looked at her strangely. "That's a suite," he explained, giving her a reassuring, professional smile.

Lily paused, not sure what to do. She had signed on for a meal in a hotel dining room, not an evening in a hotel suite.

"Would you like someone to accompany you upstairs?" the concierge asked.

"No." Lily shook her head. *Because she wasn't going to be staying. Not if it appeared an assignation was all Carson McRue wanted from her.*

Refusing however to jump to conclusions—this could all be perfectly innocent—Lily took the key and headed across the marble-floored lobby to the elevators.

Scant minutes later, she was striding down the hall to Suite 531.

Strangely enough, the door was slightly ajar. Soft music was playing inside. Lily could see vases of flowers, and a room service table set up in the middle of the room. And…Fletcher Hart lounging about on the suite's sofa. He was clad in the usual jeans and solid-colored blue work shirt, but had also thrown on a burgundy tie—whose knot had already been pulled loose—and a navy sport coat. His hair was as clean and touchably soft as always, his eyes sparkling with a mischievous light.

Lily blinked and then blinked again. This had to be a mistake. 'Cause if it wasn't, she swore to heaven above, she was really going to kill him.

Seeing her, he got to his feet and crossed lazily to the portal. "Right on time," he remarked.

Lily's pulse, already racing, upped another notch. She walked in, her handbag held like a weapon at her side. "What are you doing here?" The words were smooth as silk—her feelings were not.

"Exactly what it looks like I'm doing." Fletcher kept going until they stood toe-to-toe. "I'm filling in for your date out of the goodness of my heart."

Trying hard not to notice how much she liked the tantalizing fragrance of his aftershave, Lily held on to her temper with effort. "Where's Carson?" she asked sweetly.

Fletcher cast a completely unnecessary look over his shoulder, then turned and hooked his thumbs through the belt loops on either side of his fly. "Obviously, not here. But if you'd like to confirm that for yourself, he's staying in the penthouse on the top floor. I think they're expecting you up there, too."

Not sure whether to believe him or not, although Fletcher's expression was certainly innocent enough, Lily pivoted on her heel and stomped off, steam practically rolling out of her ears. Back to the elevators. Up to the top floor, where a hotel security officer was standing guard. She gave her name. "Oh, right. Mr. McRue's assistant is expecting you, Miss Madsen. You can go on in."

Lily headed for the double doors.

Inside, the suite was a wreck, with clothes and scripts everywhere.

Carson's raspberry-haired assistant was smoking a cigarette and talking on the phone, but she motioned Lily on in. She continued talking for another five minutes, then ended the conversation and turned to Lily. "I guess you've heard your date with Carson is off."

So Fletcher had said. "I don't understand," Lily said as calmly as she could.

"Carson had to drive out to Lexington, North Carolina, to check out some horses for the show. He's obsessed with getting one that's the right color. You know what a perfectionist he is when it comes to cinematography. Anyway, he asked me to be sure and tell you not to worry, that he would work you in at some point, before he left town."

Lily ignored the relief—that she no longer had to go through with a date she wasn't particularly interested in, and concentrated instead on her anger. "Just out of curiosity, what did Fletcher Hart have to do with all this?" she asked sweetly.

The assistant looked up from the notes she was scrawling on her clipboard. "That hunky local vet?"

"That would be the one," Lily confirmed dryly.

"He arranged it."

FLETCHER HAD FIGURED it would take Lily ten minutes to get back to him. It took her seven and a half, and when she barreled through the open doorway of the suite he had rented for the night, she looked loaded for bear. Good. 'Cause if she was angry with him, it might keep her from pursuing any of those items on that list of hers with him and he could send her home early to the safety of that big old house she lived in. Instead of where he wanted her—in his arms. He was beginning to realize this grand romantic setting he'd concocted to fulfill her dreams was a *big* mistake.

Lily tossed her evening purse down in a great show of temper. "Just where do you get off—?" she hissed.

Deciding this had the potential to get interesting—fast—Fletcher inclined his head at the portal. "You might want to close the door behind you so you don't disturb the other people on this floor."

She marched back, the hem of her dress swirling sexily around her showgirl-fine legs. "You sent him to Lexington?"

With effort, Fletcher tore his glance from her knees and pushed aside his thoughts about what it would be like to settle down between them. "He wanted to look at a lot of horses before making his decision about which stallion he was going to use for the show. It was cheaper to send him to Lexington than trailer them up and truck them all here." Not that Fletcher couldn't have arranged that, had he wanted to. Most owners he knew would have jumped at the chance to have one of their mounts appear in a prime-time TV show.

"It had to be tonight?"

Fletcher shrugged. "Carson told me he wanted this taken care of right away, and since that's what he hired me to do…" Fletcher noticed the care she had taken with her hair. Instead of leaving it down the way she usually did, she had twisted it up on the back of her head with some sort of clip. Tendrils escaped along the back of her neck and brushed at her forehead and cheeks in a very sexy way. It was the kind of hairdo that a man just itched to take down. And she looked good with her hair that way. Too good for his comfort, considering where she had been headed.

"In any case," Fletcher continued lazily, watching as her cheeks turned an even brighter pink, "sorry about your date."

Lily looked at him, a mixture of temper and resentment simmering in her pretty Carolina-blue eyes. "I bet."

"Nice dress, though." Fletcher continued his attempts to annoy the heck out of her as he moved to uncork the champagne. And he was glad Carson McRue had missed seeing Lily in it, because she was a knockout even at the end of a very long workday. All gussied up and clad in a drop-dead-sexy dress, she took his breath away. And with good reason. "It practically screams, 'Make love to me,' Fletcher concluded as the cork shot off in a spray of champagne.

The color staining her cheeks went from pink to rose in a flash.

"I don't know what you mean, Fletcher Hart."

"Then I'll explain it to you." Fletcher set the bottle back on the table and stepped toward her, determined to see out his responsibility and protect her. "For starters, you can see right through it to your slip." He indicated the black satin spaghetti-strapped sheath that hugged her surprisingly lush and womanly curves. Curves that until now had been hidden beneath sweetly sexy sundresses or pastel T-shirts and tailored khakis.

"It's not a slip." Lily swept a hand down the length of her body, her hand ghosting over the sheer floral-printed black fabric that clung to her breasts and waist before slipping over her slender hips and swirling out just above her knees. "It's part of the dress. And you're supposed to see it."

Fletcher didn't find that a help as he tilted his head to survey it. "Yeah, well all it makes a guy want to do is take off both pieces. Which I suppose was the point of your evening tonight?"

He saw it coming. Could have ducked. But didn't. 'Cause the more gallant part of him knew he deserved it, even as he continued to see red over the way she was unknowingly setting herself up to be seduced by the egotistical TV star. Or would have, had he not intervened, just in time. The slap was surprisingly powerful from such a genteel-looking woman, Fletcher noted, even as the left side of his face stung and heated.

"Finished?" he drawled. "Or do you want to do it again?"

Lily's mouth opened in a round "Oh!" Her hand dropped back to her side. "I can't believe I just did that." Her full lower lip shot out petulantly. "Even if you did have it coming."

Fletcher rubbed his still-stinging cheek. "Well, if you were me, you'd be able to believe it." Damn, that hurt.

She glared at him. "Why do you insist on interfering with my bet?" Her eyes narrowed as the next thought occurred to her. "Or, did you perchance put some money down on it, too? Money declaring I wouldn't succeed?"

Here was his chance to let her know about the bet he had made. Phrase it in such a good way that they'd both have a good laugh and figure a face-saving way out of this mess. One that would allow her to retain her considerable pride, and him to avoid earning her undying loathing, while simultaneously keeping secret the deathbed promise he had made to her grandmother Rose.

Only, he had the feeling she wouldn't forgive him. And he didn't want her angry at him forever any more than he wanted her to remain just an acquaintance or friend....

Aware she was looking at him, waiting for some disclaimer, he looked her right in the eye and said flatly, "I didn't lay money on the wager you made with the other bridesmaids."

He'd made his own bet.

And as he got more and more emotionally involved with Lily, was beginning to regret it.

"Then why?" Lily demanded, throwing up her hands and advancing on him. Not in anger this time, but with the urgent need to understand. "Why do you keep interfering in what I'm trying to do here?"

Easy, Fletcher thought, reining in his out of control emotions. "Because I don't want to see you hurt," he told her kindly.

"And you think Carson McRue will hurt me," Lily asserted sarcastically.

"Given the chance, yes." Which was why Fletcher was determined not to give Carson McRue the opportunity to cross off the items on Lily's list. Even if it meant Lily resented him forever.

Lily shook her head at him in mounting exasperation and sighed. "You are one misguided idiot, you know that?"

Fletcher grinned, glad to see her anger fading. "Does that mean you'll stay and have dinner here with me tonight?"

"No." Lily gave him a sexy, stubborn look that spoke volumes about her intent. "But I will stay long enough to make love with you."

Chapter Six

Fletcher's look of absolute shock and astonishment was everything Lily had hoped for—and more. She sashayed closer and grabbed him by the front of his shirt, knowing it was way past time he had the tables turned on him. "You don't believe me, do you?"

Fletcher's lips curved into an amused smile. "No, actually, I don't," he returned, looking as determined and devil-may-care as Lily had hoped to feel earlier.

Great. One more person who felt she didn't have it in her to be anything but prim and proper, a hopelessly naive romantic perennially on the sidelines of life. Lily admitted had it been TV star Carson McRue in the room with her now instead of the impossibly exasperating Fletcher Hart, that still would have been true. She would have been backing out—faster than a winning filly leaving the starting gate—on her promise to at least flirt with the idea of a wild, impetuous fling.

But it wasn't the questionably motivated Carson she was alone with in an elegant hotel room. It was the way too cynical Fletcher Hart. And Lily knew as much as he teased her that he wouldn't take advantage of her—he was much too gallant for that. Which was why she had to put him to the test right now.

"Sure about that?" she queried, saucily slipping past him to the open bottle of ridiculously expensive champagne on the table. Aware he was watching her—a lot more grimly now—she topped off a crystal flute and lifted it to her lips. Holding his eyes over the rim of her glass, she drank deeply of the exquisitely effervescent white wine, finishing half the glass in one gulp, the rest in the second.

"Okay, that's enough," Fletcher said, coming over to take the glass and the bottle away from her before she could pour herself a second drink. "You've proved your point now, Lily," he said as he set both aside then clasped her elbow. "I'll take you home."

Lily leaned into his easy grasp. Ignoring the quelling nature of his touch, she ran her hands over the solid warmth of his chest. "But I don't want to go home, Fletcher," she purred in the sexiest voice she could manage. She leaned forward, pressing her lips to the exposed column of his throat, in the open vee of his shirt. She felt his pulse skitter and jump, even as his body hardened all the more.

"Lily." He adapted a no-nonsense stance—legs braced, shoulders squared, head tilted down to hers— that would have been very intimidating if she allowed it.

Which, of course, Lily didn't. "Oh, shut up and just kiss me," she murmured, standing on tiptoe to better align their bodies.

And then, to her complete surprise, he did.

FLETCHER EXPECTED LILY to stop bluffing and cry uncle the moment his lips touched hers. But instead of trying to fight him off, she wreathed her arms around his neck, opened her mouth to the plundering pressure of his and let her body melt recklessly against his. He'd thought the first couple of times he had kissed her had been amazing. Sweet. Hot. Tempting beyond all reason. But those times were nothing compared to this, he thought, as he tangled his hands in the softness of her upswept hair and she dug her fingers into his shoulders and kissed him back with a wildness beyond his most erotic dreams. Her lips were soft and warm and sweet and she kissed him with absolutely nothing held back, as if he were the gallant prince of a guy she had been waiting her whole life for…as if she wanted him to make love to her then and there. Despite the way she had taunted and provoked him, despite the promises he had made to protect her at all costs, he wanted her, he realized, as his whole body tightened and flamed. And that was why this had to stop.

Reluctantly, he broke off the kiss. Stood there, searching for some inner nobility to make everything turn out right. And found it lacking as always. "Don't you have enough to regret for one night?" he asked her quietly, wishing all the while she didn't feel quite so good in his arms. That he didn't know firsthand from her wish list just how eager she was for life experience. Especially in the sexual arena…

"That's just it," she murmured in frustration. Light blue eyes shimmering wistfully, she was up on tiptoe again, innocently offering her lips up to his.

"All I've got are regrets. And I'm tired of being alone, Fletcher." Hurt from years past laced her low voice. "I'm tired of watching everyone else have fun," she confessed as she ran her palm beneath his blazer, over his chest. "Tired of seeing life pass me by."

Had she said anything else and looked at him any other way...Fletcher could easily have refused her another kiss. But the yearning in her soft eyes and even softer voice had him ignoring his better judgment and capitulating once again.

Lily was right, Fletcher rationalized. Through no fault of her own, the freedom Lily should have had in her late teens and early twenties had been taken from her, and for far too long she had been closeted up in a life chosen for her.

She wanted adventure. Passion. Excitement. Right now she was looking for him to give it to her. What was the harm in a little kissing, he wondered, particularly if it didn't lead to anything else...?

Lily hadn't expected Fletcher to kiss her at all, never mind like this. He made her feel as if she were the only woman on earth for him, and vice versa. How could she possibly go back to the loneliness of her life now? For so long she'd had walls around her heart, and she wanted Fletcher Hart to be the man to tear them down once and for all.

Needing, wanting, to be closer still, she wove her fingers through his honey-brown hair and opened her mouth to the demanding pressure of his. He tasted so good, Lily thought, as his tongue plundered deep and their kiss took on an even more urgent quality.

Her breasts pressed against the solid wall of his chest, and, lower still, she felt the hot urgency of his arousal. Desire welled up inside her, a river of unbridled passion, and her knees went weak. She had never experienced such deliciously wanton kisses, such intense aching need, and that alone was enough to make her want to see where this clinch would lead. Besides marking an end to her innocence, would making love with Fletcher change things between them in other ways, too?

Or would Fletcher remain as cynical—and aloof—as ever? And it was the thought that he might not acknowledge that something very special was happening between them that had her coming to her senses. She was in the market for a satisfying, life-changing love affair, not a broken heart.

As she broke the kiss and pulled away, Fletcher looked stunned by the abrupt change in her mood. And not the least bit happy about it. "Now what?" he demanded gruffly.

"Now," Lily said, "it's time for me to say good-night to you and go home."

"WHERE ARE JANEY and Thad registered again?" Fletcher asked his mother the next morning when he stopped by the Wedding Inn on his way to work.

Helen Hart turned away from the outdoor wedding being set up for later in the day. It was her busy season. The inn was still booked every day in August with at least one wedding, sometimes two. At fifty-six, she was a little more curvaceous than she had been in his youth, but with her short red hair, fair skin and amber eyes, she was still one of the prettiest women around. As well as resolutely single. Although she'd had plenty of invitations, Helen hadn't dated anyone since his dad's death twenty years ago.

Helen motioned for the wedding arbor in the gardens to be placed a little farther to the left—given the semi-circular arrangement of the three hundred fifty white folding chairs—then turned back to him. "We went over this the other night, Fletcher, at the barbecue."

Fletcher shrugged. "I've had a lot on my mind."

Helen wrote the name of several stores down on a piece of paper, removed it from her clipboard and handed it to him. "So I've heard," she said dryly.

Fletcher stuck it in the pocket of his sage-green shirt. "What does that mean?"

His mother turned to him, giving him the full benefit of her knowing amber gaze, before she sighed. "What's this I hear about you trying to saddle Lily Madsen with a dog she doesn't want?"

Guilt rose up inside him. It wasn't like him to be so manipulative. But then, it wasn't like him to be so interested in any one woman, either. He palmed his chest in self-defense. "Hey, she volunteered to take Spartacus."

Helen scoffed. "Only after you arranged to send the poor mutt to the pound. Why didn't you ask your nephew Christopher to care for him? Or didn't an arrangement like that suit your purposes?"

Leave it to his mother to hit the nail right on the head. "I don't know what you mean."

"I think you do. I think you've been using that

poor dog to keep Lily occupied so she won't pursue that TV star who is in town filming location shots. What's his name? Carson McNally?''

''McRue, Mom. And I don't know where you got such a silly idea.''

''Mmm-hmm.'' Helen regarded him skeptically as she gave the thumbs-up sign to the new location of the arbor. ''What's going on with you and Lily?''

Fletcher tried to look as innocent as Lily. ''Nothing.'' *Except a few kisses,* he amended silently. *And the burning desire, on my part anyway, to make hot passionate love that lasts all night and well into the next day.*

Helen sighed and walked over to check on the bandstand being erected in the grass, leaving Fletcher to follow at will. ''I didn't buy that excuse when you were ten. I'm not buying it now. She's a sweet girl, Fletcher.''

Tell me something I don't know.

''She's been through a lot. Growing up without her parents, sacrificing her teenage years to nurse her grandmother Rose through that long illness and then grieving the loss of her only family.''

Fletcher set his mouth grimly. ''You don't have to tell me Lily needs protection from a guy like Carson McRue.''

Nodding her approval, Helen headed back toward the white brick inn. ''Is that what you're doing? Protecting her?''

Fletcher paused, knowing he had to tell someone or he was going to implode. ''I don't have a choice,

Mom. And if you mention any of what I'm about to tell you to anyone…''

Helen escorted Fletcher into her office and shut the door firmly behind her so they could speak in private. She dropped her clipboard and perched on the edge of her desk. ''I won't tell a soul. You know that. Now, what is going on, Fletcher?''

Fletcher dropped into a chair and stretched his long legs out in front of him. ''I promised Rose before she died that I would look out for Lily.''

Helen mulled that over. ''Why did she ask *you?*''

''I don't know.'' Fletcher shook his head in silent regret. ''I told her I wasn't the one to fulfill her request. I mean, I'm just not a trustworthy kind of guy when it comes to something like that.''

''Heavens, Fletcher! Tell me you haven't taken advantage of Lily Madsen!''

Not yet…

''I know you're cynical and not prone to any sort of responsibility not connected with your vet practice, but—''

Fletcher held up both hands in a gesture of surrender, before his mother made him feel any worse. ''It's not as easy as it sounds, Mom. Lily really wants to go out with this guy.''

Understanding lit Helen's eyes. ''Because of the bet she made?''

Fletcher swore silently to himself. ''You heard about that, too?''

''As well as the one you made.''

Fletcher clenched his hands on the arms of the

chair. His bet was supposed to be secret. "Who told you?" he demanded gruffly.

"No one. I just happened to overhear two of your brothers talking yesterday. They didn't know I was there, and I didn't let on that I'd heard what they were saying."

"But obviously you disapprove," Fletcher summarized.

Helen reproached him seriously. "You cannot play with someone's heart like this."

Figuring he'd heard enough, Fletcher stood. "No hearts involved," Fletcher said lightly. Not yet, anyway.

His mother scoffed, the knowing look back in her eyes. "You're kidding yourself if you think that."

LILY AND SPARTACUS WERE almost ready to leave for work that morning when the sleek black limousine pulled up in front of her home. She watched in disbelief as Carson McRue got out of the car, a big bouquet of yellow roses in hand. They weren't the best quality, Lily noted but the presentation was elaborate.

As Carson mounted the steps to the covered portico, Spartacus went wild, barking and jumping. "Okay, okay." Lily patted Spartacus on the back of the head. "You can stop protecting me. I want this guy here." If only to tell him she had sort of changed her mind about going out with him, bet or no bet. She'd made enough of a fool of herself lately, throwing herself at Fletcher Hart. She didn't need to add any more romantic nonsense to the mix.

Holding on to Spartacus's collar with one hand, she opened the door.

Carson stopped, his hand on the bell. Spartacus began to growl.

Carson tensed and stepped back. "What's with Fido?" he asked, but the jovial note in his voice did not match the annoyance in his pale green eyes.

"He's just feeling protective," Lily explained while Spartacus strained against her hold. Continuing to struggle, the dog's feet moved rapidly across the wood floor. But he was going nowhere fast, thanks to Lily's tight grip on him. It looked like a parody of a Fred Flintstone cartoon.

"I meant the socks on his paws. What's that about?"

"Uh—long story," Lily said as a low, fierce growl came out of Spartacus's throat. She couldn't believe how fierce he sounded.

"Why don't you put the dog up?" Carson asked genially.

"Good idea." Lily took Spartacus by the collar and guided him over to the study at the front of the house. She pushed him inside, gave the stay command and shut the door.

The growls continued behind the portal.

Expression tense, Carson handed her the flowers. "Listen, I just came over to apologize for last night."

"Did you get the horse you wanted for the filming?"

"None of the ones that vet arranged to have me look at were right. They were all way too docile. But I did find this stallion that was something. Just exactly the look I had in mind. So we're going to use him.''

Alarm bells sounded in Lily's head. An unruly stallion could be a danger under the best of circumstances. ''Did Fletcher okay that?''

Carson pressed his lips together grimly. ''Fletcher Hart has nothing to say about what we do or don't do on the set.''

''I thought he was advising the production in a professional capacity.''

He made a disrespectful sound. ''That's just to satisfy the animal rights people, keep them off our back. It has nothing to do with the reality of filming. But enough about that.'' The hundred-watt smile was back on his face. ''I want to make up to you for our canceled date last night. So how about it? Can you go out with me tonight? The jet is at the Raleigh airport. We can have dinner in any city you want. Go out dancing all night, or just sit up talking, if you want.''

If Lily didn't know better, she would think Carson had read her list and was ready to provide her with all the romantic adventure and excitement she needed. ''Don't you have to film tomorrow?'' she asked, not sure why she was suddenly so reluctant to be alone with him.

''Yeah. And the next couple of days after that. Then we're out of here. So what do you say?''

''Oh, I wish I could,'' Lily fibbed. Because thanks to Fletcher Hart, and the very genuine way he had kissed her and held her in his arms, she now had zero interest in going out with anyone as superficial as Carson McRue. "But I've got a bachelorette party to attend tonight."

Carson looked unimpressed. "Skip it."

"I can't. I'm a bridesmaid in the wedding."

"So? Tell 'em you're going to be with me. They'll get over it."

"I can't do that. Janey Hart is one of my very best friends."

Carson undressed Lily with his eyes. "She'd understand," he said softly.

A shiver of distaste rippled down Lily's spine. "And I have to work tomorrow."

"No problem. You can sleep on the jet, both to and from dinner." Carson gave her a lascivious wink. "I have a *very* comfortable bed on the jet."

Lily just bet he did. "Thanks," she said, "but I really can't."

FLETCHER DIDN'T HEAR from Lily at all that day. A half-dozen times he picked up the phone to call her, to apologize for waylaying her date and allowing things to get out of hand the night before, and then put it right back down again. There was no point in telling her anything that wasn't absolutely true. He didn't want her going out with Carson, and the only thing he regretted about their encounter was that he had let it end with only kisses when all he really wanted to do was take her to bed. Make her his. Not just for the moment, the day, the week, but for always. And how crazy was that? He wasn't the marrying kind. Not at all. But Lily had him thinking about rings on their fingers and vows that would last forever and shared spaces. And Fletcher sensed, as he headed into the private sports bar where Thad Lantz's bachelor party was being held, it was only going to get worse in the days ahead.

"Don't you look like you need a drink," Dylan Hart observed.

"He probably heard about what the gals are doing tonight and is upset," Mac said.

The look on his law-and-order brother's face gave Fletcher pause.

"The bachelorette party is tonight, too," Cal Hart explained.

"So?" Fletcher shrugged. "What are they going to do? Make a wedding veil out of toilet paper and stick it on the bride's head?"

"We wish," Joe said, scowling. Since becoming Emma Donovan's husband, he had really settled down.

Fletcher helped himself to some peanuts from the bucket on the table. "What are they doing?"

More looks that told Fletcher he was the only one there in the dark. "Rite of passage," Joe said finally. "They're going to a bar near the State campus."

Fletcher started to have a very bad feeling about all this as Dylan continued filling him in. "Lily has a bet to pay off. You know, the one about dating Carson McRue?"

Hope flared in Fletcher's heart. "She's given up on that?"

Thad nodded. "Apparently he came by and asked her out again for tonight and she turned him down flat," Thad said.

So why were all the men in the wedding party looking so grim? "That's good, isn't it?" Fletcher asked. Lord knew he was relieved.

"Not unless she actually agrees to go out with you, which I must point out she hasn't done yet." Cal studied him with a physician's trained eye. "Has she?"

"She will," Fletcher predicted.

All the men in the wedding party buried their heads in their drinks. "What?" Fletcher demanded. Clearly, they all knew something he didn't.

Mac turned back to him. His expression was grim. "You don't know what Lily Madsen wagered she would do if she lost. Do you?"

LILY AND THE OTHER female participants of Janey Hart's wedding party got out of the white stretch limo in front of the nightclub. Just nine o'clock, but the place was already packed with college kids. Music roared from the inside. Above the front door a big hot pink banner rippled in the wind, advertising the nightly contest that drew the wildest, most uninhibited women around. And tonight, thanks to the bet she had just lost, Lily was going to become one of them.

"Gonna enter the contest?" the bouncer asked with a cheerful wink as Lily walked through the door.

Feeling as if she were on her death march, she nodded. She had purposefully timed this so she wouldn't have time to reconsider and back out. Blessedly, the events were about to begin. As the evening's host—a popular deejay from a local radio station—got up on stage, Lily looked at some of the pitchers on the tables. "I'm really going to need a margarita. A pitcher of margaritas."

"Margaritas are what got you into this situation in the first place," Susan said.

Janey grabbed Lily's arm, suddenly as much a mother to Lily as she was to her twelve-year-old son, Christopher. "You know you really don't have to do this, Lily. We'll all put our heads together and think of something else."

Lily thought of the boasts she had made and shook her head stubbornly. "I'm not chickening out. A bet's a bet. I said I'd do it. I will."

Hannah rolled her eyes. "You were three sheets to the wind at the time!"

"Doesn't matter," Lily said grimly. Maybe this would teach her not to *ever* behave like such a fool again, lost teen years or not.

The microphone came on as the music cranked up even louder. "Okay, ladies. Let's go," the announcer said. "Everyone who's gonna participate up on stage."

Lily flushed, already feeling hideously embarrassed.

"And remember the rules. No bras. If you're wearing any kind of undie, you're disqualified. Okay?"

Lily swallowed and reached under her plain white T-shirt to unfasten the clasp. She was already beetred and she hadn't even done anything yet.

"Uh-oh," Hannah said, looking toward the door.

Susan Hart scowled as she turned her gaze in the same direction. "What are *they* doing here?" she demanded, looking no happier than Lily to see they had a hometown audience.

Lily gulped as she saw all five of the Hart brothers and Janey's fiancé, Thad, coming toward them, Fletcher in the lead. Clad in the usual snug jeans, custom-fitted boots and solid-colored cotton shirt, Fletcher looked so ruggedly handsome and sexy, she felt herself go weak in the knees.

As he crossed to her side and took her by the arm, the air left her lungs in one big whoosh. "I don't care what bet you made—" he pushed the words through clenched teeth "—you're out of here."

Lily resented his taking charge of and imposing restrictions on *her* life. Wasn't that what she had been trying to get away from? Ignoring the flare of his nostrils and the take-no-guff-set of his broad shoulders, she folded her arms in front of her, and glared up at him. "You don't have any say about what I do or don't do, Fletcher Hart!" she shot back furiously, digging in her heels.

"The hell I don't." Still holding her tightly, he leaned down until they were nose to nose. "The only one ever going to see you in a wet T-shirt is me."

Chapter Seven

"Now what?" Lily demanded, as they exited the Wild Girls Only nightclub.

Fletcher tightened his grip on her elbow as they rounded the corner to the parking lot where he had left his pickup truck. "I'm taking you for a frozen custard."

Pretending she wasn't relieved to have been hustled out of a seedy place she had never wanted to venture into in the first place, Lily propped her fists on her hips and squared off with him contentiously. "Why?" she demanded as her newfound recklessness took over once again and urged her to explore life to its limits.

Fletcher took one of her wrists in his hand and forced her to continue walking away from the raucous activity of the college bars. "Because every time I got in trouble and my dad needed to talk to me, he took me out for ice cream."

Lily scowled, as they rounded a corner at the end of the block and the noise abruptly died down. She hated the fact Fletcher looked so at ease when she was still tied up in knots. "You're not my father."

And I'm not in trouble. Not yet anyway. Although if he kept looking at her that way, as if he wanted to keep everyone else at bay, all bets about that were off, as well....

"Well, right now I'm the closest thing you've got to a male protector in your life," Fletcher countered dryly. He continued to look at her in his very sexy, very determined way. "What were you thinking anyway?" He sighed his exasperation loudly. "Going into a place like that?"

The college bar had been more raucous than Lily had expected, but she'd be darned if she admitted that to him. She shrugged as if she did wild and crazy things like that all the time. "It was part of the bet."

Fletcher shook his head in silent reproach. The set of his lips was grim again as they reached his pickup truck. "So I heard."

Lily leaned against the passenger door. Fletcher adapted a no-nonsense stance—legs braced apart, one arm stretched out beside her and braced on the roof of the cab, the other resting on his waist—that would have been very intimidating had she allowed it. She didn't.

Lily lifted her chin another notch, daring him to try and chastise her for living her life to the fullest in whatever cockeyed way she chose. "How did you find out the terms?" she demanded.

Fletcher narrowed his eyes, his glance reminding her she had almost done something she would surely have regretted, newfound freedom or not. "Joe knew. And so did Thad."

So Emma spilled the beans to her husband, and

Janey had told her fiancé. Knowing how close the two women were to the men they loved, Lily wasn't surprised. Nor did she mind. Especially when she herself longed to have someone she could confide everything to. Someone like Fletcher Hart? If only he were the marrying kind…instead of someone who had long maintained he only had the inclination and energy for one lifetime commitment—to his work.

"They were clearly worried," Fletcher continued pragmatically.

Somehow, Lily wasn't surprised to find the whole Hart clan was now looking out for her. It seemed if she had the support of one, she had the backing of the entire family. "And disapproving, as well, I guess?" Lily said lightly as she moved away from the lock.

Fletcher opened the door and helped her inside. "That, too." He looked at her again as he slid behind the wheel. "Now what?" he asked, eluding to her deepening scowl.

"I still have to pay off my bet."

"Not that way you're not," he said firmly. And the look on his face told her he meant it. If he even caught wind of her going near that place again, he'd be right there to stop her. The thought was as comforting as it was annoying.

Not that she really wanted to take off her bra, get hosed down and then have the quality of her breasts voted on, for heaven's sake.

Honestly, Lily thought, as she buried her face in her hands. What had she been thinking? Was being exuberantly youthful worth that kind of humiliation, just so you could someday look back and remember when you had been wild and uninhibited? Or was there a better way? A way she had yet to discover?

Fletcher drove a couple miles away from campus, then pulled into the parking lot of the frozen custard shop. At almost ten there was still a line at all the customer windows of the outdoor stand. The picnic tables scattered about were full of customers, too.

Lily watched him get out of the truck but made no move to follow him. Maybe it was time they called a halt to this evening. She really didn't think she wanted a lecture from him on the error of her ways, anyway. No point in him telling her what she already knew.

He came around to her side anyway and held the passenger door. "What kind of custard do you want?" he said.

"I want to go home," Lily said quietly.

His golden-brown eyes filled with compassion and he flashed her one of his sexiest smiles. "Just take a look at the menu." He clasped her hand. Together they walked over to the glass windows that served as the order area for the frozen-custard stand. Lily didn't mind the lineup. It gave her time to study the extensive menu painted on the boards above the windows, and consider how hungry she really was. And since Fletcher was paying…

As they moved away from the window with their delectable sundaes he guided her to a low brick wall that edged the grassy area surrounding the custard stand. Making sure they were out of earshot of everyone else, he sat down and stretched his long legs out in front of him. Lily sat down, too, making sure there was a good distance between them. Which, of course, he promptly closed simply by sliding toward her. "So, back to what we were talking about," he stated casually.

As if he didn't know. Lily cast her glance at the stars gleaming in the sky overhead. "Your youthful travails."

"No." He edged closer so their sides were touching in one long electrified line. "Yours."

Lily shifted back a little and then turned so her bent knee was touching the rock-hard muscle in his blue-jean clad thigh. She sent him a level look, aware her heart was racing again. "I lost the bet, Fletcher. I had to pay up."

He left the spoon in his mouth and paused to consider that. "You've still got time to get a date with Carson McRue."

Lily scoffed and met his too-innocent gaze head-on. "Ha! Not if you have anything to do about it."

He grinned wickedly.

"I notice you're not denying it," Lily observed, feeling the heat of excitement climb to her face.

Fletcher lifted his broad shoulders in an unapologetically lazy shrug. "I never pretended to *want* you to go out with him."

Lily refused to let herself think what that might mean. Save the fact Fletcher Hart was the most exasperating, ornery man she had ever met in her life. "Then why didn't you let me go through with the contest tonight?" she asked, aware the heat welling up inside her was nothing compared to the heat in his gaze.

"Like I said..." All the humor left his face, replaced by something much more dangerous. His voice dropped another seductive notch. "I don't want anyone seeing you in a wet T-shirt but me."

Lily swallowed at the rough note of possession and protectiveness in his voice. "And what does that mean?"

He shifted toward her and nudged her knee playfully with his. "What do you think it means?"

Lily felt a melting sensation in her middle, completely at odds with the emotional territory she was attempting to stake out. "That just because we've kissed a few times and verbally sparred even more that you're suddenly interested in me?" she asked lightly, pretending she wasn't playing with fire here.

His expression turned serious. "Not suddenly," he said quietly, offering her a bite of his custard.

As the creamy chocolate melted on her tongue, Lily lifted a curious brow.

He favored her with a sexy half smile, his eyes roving her face. "I've always had a thing for you," he told her softly. "From way back."

This was news. Lily caught her breath.

Trying to act normal, she spooned up some mint-chocolate chip for him. "You never acted like it."

He acknowledged this with a dip of his head, his eyes never leaving hers. "You were too young," he said quietly. "Five years is a big difference in your teens and early twenties. Then by the time the playing ground was more level, and you were old enough that I could consider asking you out, you were going through too much with your grandmother and her illness to get serious about anyone.''

Lily's heart took a triple leap. With effort, she tried to keep herself from making too much of his unexpected confession. She swallowed the knot of emotion in her throat. ''Did you want me to get serious about you?''

''Well, I didn't want to be one of the legions of guys you dated once or twice and then never saw again, if that's what you're asking.''

Her Ice Princess of Holly Springs rep reared its ugly head again, gained from years of being too polite to turn anyone down—no matter how ill suited they were to her—when she was asked out. Grandmother Rose had told her to go out at least once with anyone who asked her…because you never knew… The love of your life could be right there in front of your eyes. So Lily had done that, working her way through many of the single guys in Holly Springs. But there had never been any sparks, and after one date, sometimes two, they both always knew that.

Hence her reputation…

Well deserved, Lily supposed. Until now.

Now, there were sparks…. With the man she had never dreamed she would be kissing, or talking to on a regular basis, or sitting here sharing sweethearts and secrets…

She knew what this meant to her. Everything. But what did it mean to him? As she looked deep into his eyes, she couldn't honestly say. So she looked away. ''I never meant to hurt anyone's feelings,'' she confessed softly, wanting Fletcher to understand this much about her. "In fact, I tried really hard not to do so." That was why she'd said yes to dates maybe she shouldn't have said yes to and ended things as soon as it was clear there wasn't any real chemistry.

"I know that," he said softly. "I've done the same thing and ended up with the same kind of pretty much undeserved love-'em-and-leave-'em reputation."

They were quiet again, but it was a companionable silence now. "Is that why you've been kissing me?" Lily asked finally, putting her empty paper cup and spoon aside. "And chasing me? Because you've decided it's time to make your move?"

Briefly, emotion flashed in his eyes, but it was gone before Lily could decipher it. He released a lengthy sigh. Looked serious and adult and responsible again. "I'm worried about you, Lily," he said finally, all traces of the ardent suitor disappearing as quickly and inevitably as they had appeared. His lips thinned. "And I'm not the only one. You haven't been yourself since your grandmother Rose died last year. First you were so withdrawn you barely cracked a smile. You just seemed to be going through the motions of your everyday life."

Lily really didn't want to talk about this. She rolled her eyes. "So I was like a Stepford florist, is that it?"

Ignoring her sarcasm, he continued searching her face. "Then the past few weeks you've been...kind of...I don't know. Unusually adventurous, I guess."

Lily felt the heat creeping back into her cheeks.

She told herself it was the unduly warm temperature of the August evening. ''That's a nice way to put it.''

His glance scanned her, taking in the white T-shirt and the tight jeans she had bought as a twenty-fifth birthday present to herself. ''You have to admit you haven't been acting like yourself,'' he said softly.

Lily rubbed the toe of her sandal across the grass and felt the soft blades tickle her bare toes. Another first. Grandmother Rose had always insisted Lily wear stockings or silk socks of some sort beneath her trousers because true ladies didn't show their bare feet off in public. It just wasn't proper.

Wanting—needing—Fletcher to see where she was coming from, Lily confessed emotionally, ''That's just the point, Fletcher. I don't know who I am. I've never had the chance to find out. I've just been so focused on everyone and everything else.'' Eyes burning, Lily shook her head. ''I missed that time during my college years where I should have been exploring all the different facets of my personality. I was forced to grow up and be the person Grandmother Rose needed me to be. I never went to the beach with my friends and just hung out. Never drank too many margaritas or dated anyone I really shouldn't, or had wild and crazy se—''

''Sex?'' Fletcher guessed where she was going.

Lily clapped a hand over her mouth. She couldn't believe she had almost said that. She ducked her head, blushing furiously, unable to meet his eyes. She rubbed her foot across the velvety grass again. ''You know what I mean.''

"Yeah," he said slowly, leaning forward to rest a companionable hand on her knee. "I think I do." He squeezed her thigh. "And I think it's something we can fix readily enough, without you partaking in a wet-T-shirt competition."

"What are you planning?" Lily demanded, looking every bit as excited as Fletcher wanted her to be.

"Exactly what you'd think." Fletcher flashed her a mischievous smile, glad he finally knew what the problem was because now he knew how to fix it, too. "A way for you to get in touch with your inner bad girl." He lifted his brows in taunting fashion, leaned closer still and settled his hand on her thigh in unmistakable sexual intent. "Unless, of course, you're chicken."

Lily quivered beneath his touch, looking as if she wanted him to lead her astray, even as she wanted to keep guarding her heart from any damage he might inflict.

But Fletcher knew he wasn't going to hurt Lily. Rather, he was determined to keep her from getting hurt.

"Am I going to like this?" she asked, even as he took charge of their trash with one hand and helped her to her feet with the other.

Already guiding her toward the parking lot, Fletcher leaned down to teasingly whisper in her ear, "There's only one way to find out. Isn't there?"

He opened her door for her, then climbed behind the wheel. Moments later he dialed the cell phone mounted on the dash, leaving it on speakerphone so Lily would see he planned no secrets between them.

Two rings later, a male voice answered. "Cal Hart here."

"Hey, Cal." Fletcher smiled over at Lily. "It's Fletcher. The party going okay?" They could hear chatter and laughter and country-and-western music in the background.

"We've sort of combined operations," Cal said above the din of clinking glasses and more laughter. "Where are you?"

"With Lily." Fletcher took her hand and pressed the back of it to his lips. "Say, mind if I…uh, borrow your orchard tonight?"

Cal's chuckle rumbled over the cell phone connection. "I'm not even going to inquire," he promised dryly.

"Thanks." Fletcher released Lily's hand and cut the connection before his brother could ask him anything more.

Lily raked the edge of her teeth across the plumpness of her lower lip. "Why did you ask him that?"

Pausing only momentarily to note how pretty she looked in the glow of the street lamps overhead, Fletcher backed out of the space. He drove out of the lot, anticipating the evening ahead. "So Cal wouldn't pull in to his driveway, see someone parked out there and think he needed to call the sheriff's department on the trespassers out there. Unless, of course, you'd like someone to call the sheriff on us, just to make it more exciting." He waggled his eyebrows at her playfully. "In which case I can pick a few places where we'd be likely to get picked up pretty darn quick."

Lily's eyes widened as she clapped a hand across her heart, unknowingly drawing his attention to the soft round breasts enticingly encased in snug white cotton. Which in turn made him wonder what she had on beneath, since he had seen the transparent wisps of lace drying in the laundry room. "You're taking me parking?" she gasped, amazed.

"Sure." Fletcher shrugged as if it were no big deal, when to him it *was* a very big deal. "Why not?" As they stopped at the next traffic light, he looked at her playfully. "You ever been?"

She shrank in her seat even as her eyes glowed with excitement. "Well, no."

Fletcher reached over and patted her knee again. "Trust me," he reassured her, "it's a lot more fun than a wet-T-shirt competition."

Lily bit her lip again, her cheeks growing ever pinker. "You're awfully sure of yourself, aren't you?" she asked.

Fletcher just smiled.

"I DIDN'T THINK you were going to do it," Lily said a short while later as Fletcher turned his pickup into the country home owned by Cal Hart and his away-on-a-fellowship physician wife.

Fletcher drove right past the home Cal was reno-vating in what little spare time he had and continued on down the gravel lane that went past the barn to the sprawling orchard beyond. Lily guessed it encompassed about ten acres. There were more apple, pear, peach and cherry trees on the property than she'd ever imagined possible.

"Why? Would you rather go cow-tipping?" he asked her in mock seriousness. "'Cause we could do that. I even know a trick or two...."

Lily held up a hand, feeling a sort of perverse amusement as well as ever-escalating excitement at what they were about to do. "I bet you do. And no, I don't want to go cow-tipping, Fletcher." As far as she was concerned, there were some teenage adventures better left unexplored. That was one of them.

"Then parking it is." His lip took on a sensual slant as he drove slowly down the gravel lane that wound around through the rows and rows of trees. He took his hand off her knee to gesture expansively. "Pick your spot."

Lily wondered just how far he was planning to take this. "You pick since this was your idea."

He flashed her a crooked smile as he stopped the truck abruptly and cut the motor with a decisive flip of the ignition switch. "I don't hear you protesting all that much."

Lily swallowed hard as he reached behind the seat to pull out a lantern-style flashlight. He switched it on, and the beam illuminated the moonlit sky to the romantic aura of a dimly lit restaurant. "That's 'cause I'm curious," she said, watching as he pulled out a bucket and a plastic trash bag.

He got out of the truck. She joined him at the front of the truck. "Mind if we pick some fruit first?"

She watched him set the battery-powered lantern on the hood of the pickup. "You're kidding."

"No." He paused to line the farm bucket with the plastic bag, then looked up at her in all earnestness.

"Unless you'd rather get down and dirty right away...."

Lily leaned against the front of the pickup, the bumper hitting her just above the knees. "You're making this oh-so-romantic." Which maybe was his purpose? To discourage her? But as he looked down at her in the soft glow of the lantern and the moonlight filtering down through the trees, it appeared discouragement was the last thing on his mind.

"Ah, so it's romance you want," he theorized softly, dropping the bucket on the ground and sifting both hands through her hair. "Not just hot, wild, sex."

Actually, she wanted that, too. So much. But not as part of some experiment to quell her lust for passion and adventure. Ignoring the heat emanating from his body, she murmured in a low tone rife with exasperation, "Fletcher."

"Hmm?" Looking as confused as she was about what was going on between them, he reached out and ever so gently, tentatively, touched her cheek.

"What are you doing?" *Besides making me want you as never before, even if this isn't about love, or is ever going to be....*

Brought abruptly back to his senses by her tone, Fletcher emitted a long, lust-filled sigh as he picked up the bucket again and stepped away from her. "Exactly what it looks like," Fletcher replied. "I'm trying to keep me and you out of trouble against all my baser instincts."

Lily caught him by the shirtfront and hauled him against her. "Maybe I like those baser instincts," she said, her heart pounding as she took charge of the situation once again.

Fletcher ran his hands down the length of her sides, eliciting tingles wherever he touched. "Baby, you haven't seen those baser instincts."

But she would like to see them. So much, now that they were alone again and doing something that felt so deliciously…forbidden. She took his hand and kissed the back of it, loving the warm, masculine texture of his skin. "So why did you bring me out here?"

He turned their entwined fingers around and kissed the underside of her wrist with his open mouth and the butterfly touch of his tongue. "To give you the chance to be bad even though I think you'd rather be good."

He knew her so well. Trying to do some of the things she had done tonight was like trying to wear a pair of shoes that just didn't fit. No matter what you did, what pose you took on, you were never going to be comfortable.

"And I don't want to see you do anything else you're going to have to regret," he said quietly, serious now, letting their joined hands fall back to their sides before disengaging them altogether.

"Like my birthday bet," Lily guessed around the sudden tightness of her throat, the disappointment in her heart. Once again, the noble side of Fletcher had taken charge, the side that wanted to protect and shelter her. Just as Grandmother Rose had done.

Painfully honest, his eyes touched hers. "That's right."

Her emotions in turmoil, Lily pushed away from the front of the truck and began walking through the orchard. "What would you know about having things to regret?" She flung the words over her shoulders.

As far as she could see, Fletcher might be cynical as could be, when it came to his personal relationships, but he'd never done anything he'd regretted. Except maybe go on a date with someone he should never have said yes to in the first place.

"Oh, you'd be surprised," he drawled, catching up, wrapping an arm around her waist and tugging her near.

"Tell me," Lily said, adjusting her steps to mesh with his.

For a long moment, she thought he wasn't going to answer, then he tightened his fingers on hers and let the lantern fall on a nice patch of grass. He sank down on the grass and watched as she did the same. "There was the last time I ever saw my dad."

Lily stretched out beside Fletcher, so they were lying face to face in the moonlight. "What happened?"

Fletcher ran his hand over the grass between them. "He had taken me out for ice cream and I basically wasn't speaking to him." Fletcher looked into her eyes and this time it wasn't hard for her to read his thoughts. "He wanted to talk to me alone about my grief over our dog's death. He knew I felt responsible, and he wanted to make it better. But I didn't give him the chance. I just turned away, demanded he take me home, and he did." As he paused, Lily felt a bond growing between them that she never could have envisioned, and her heart swelled at their growing closeness. "The next day he left on a business trip." Fletcher's lips tightened sadly. "His plane crashed and I never saw him again."

Lily touched his arm compassionately. "Oh, Fletcher."

He tensed at her touch and rolled over onto his back. Throwing an arm across his eyes, he continued in a rusty-sounding voice. "So you see, I've had a lifetime of regrets since I was ten." He paused, shook his head, let his arm fall. "It's no way to live. Believe me."

Lily continued stroking his arm. "Your mother must've told you that your dad understood your reluctance to talk about what had happened, that you were just a kid, acting on your unhappiness."

Fletcher turned his glance away, but not before Lily caught a glimpse of his pain.

"My mother doesn't know. I never told her."

Lily blinked, stunned. The Harts seemed so close. She couldn't imagine any secrets between them. "But surely—"

Fletcher cut her off with a shake of his head and continued wearily. "I don't think she and my dad had a chance to talk that night because when Dad and I got back from the ice cream place there was some plumbing crisis going on. One of the bathrooms was flooding, and by the time they got it cleaned up, it was late."

"So you never told anyone what happened between you and your dad that night?"

Rolling to face her once again, Fletcher shook his head. "Why make anyone else in the family feel worse than they already did over losing him?" he asked in a low, brooding voice. "Besides, my mother was a wreck. She had six kids, limited life insurance, no job. She didn't know how she was going to get by. She had to sell the house up north and move back here to be near family. Then her parents died shortly thereafter and left her the Wedding Inn."

"Only, it wasn't a business back then," Lily recalled.

"Just an overly large home with flagging upkeep and impossible taxes. But she saw the potential and began working her heart out. We all helped and..."

"The more time passed..." Lily guessed where Fletcher was going with this.

"The more pointless it was to talk about what had happened between me and my dad," Fletcher concluded, looking at her as if he wanted—needed—her to understand. "Anyway, since then I've tried really hard not to give people the impression I'm anything more than exactly what I am," he concluded cynically, the devil-may-care note back in his voice.

Lily lay on her stomach in the soft grass, her chin propped on her upraised palm. "Which is what, Fletcher? A wonderful vet and even more wonderful human being?"

He shook his head, not apologizing. Making no excuses. Just telling it like it was—in his opinion, anyway. "The kind of guy who—at least in his personal life—has a talent for doing and or saying the wrong thing. *Every time.*"

And she was part of his personal life, Lily knew. Which might not bode well for them as a couple, unless she could change his mind about this. "You're selling yourself short," she told him gruffly.

He tugged on a lock of her hair. "What would you know about it?"

Lily brushed off his hand and scrambled to a sitting position. Determined to be serious about this. "I know that when it comes to me and my problems you say and do the right thing every time, Fletcher Hart."

He caught her by the waist and the next thing Lily knew she was on her back again, Fletcher sprawled over her. "You consider the right thing bringing you out here to get hot and heavy with me?" he murmured as he pushed her knees apart with one of his and slid between them, settling more deeply between her spread thighs.

Oh, my. This was turning very sensual, very fast. Lily braced both her forearms against the hardness of his chest, loving the warmth and strength and danger of him. "You haven't made out with me," she taunted back just as lightly. *Yet.*

The wicked grin was back, more devastating than ever. "Oh, I think we can remedy that." He kissed one corner of her mouth, then the other.

Lily's plan to make him work for it was already disintegrating. Her lips parted slightly and she let her head fall back. "Do you?"

"Oh, yeah." He took her forearms, put them around his shoulders and dropped his head. Then he took her mouth in a long, hot, searing kiss. Lily had never been wanted quite this way, never wanted this way. She arched up against him, needing, yearning, until there was only the fierce reckless pressure of his lips on hers, the strong warm cage of his arms, the demanding pressure of his body draped over hers. She felt like his woman and he kissed her until she felt like swooning, then kissed her some more until she clung to him and whimpered low in her throat. Until she kissed him back the way he was kissing her, with every fiber of his being. With a low groan of pleasure she tangled her fingers in his hair and brought him closer yet, straining toward him until it was clear that if they kept this up they would have a decision to make.

His breaths coming as raggedly as hers, Fletcher broke the kiss and lifted his head. Arm anchored around her waist, he rolled so he was beneath her, the proof of his desire as unmistakable as her own. He stroked his thumb across her lower lip, the arch of her brow, the line of her cheek. "Lily," he murmured with all the tenderness she had ever dreamed, "I want to make love to you."

Her body was throbbing everywhere. His was, too. "I want to make love to you, too," Lily whispered, reaching for the hem of her T-shirt.

His expression determined, Fletcher caught her wrist before she could go any further. "No way is our first time together going to be here."

Chapter Eight

"So much for being out with a bad boy," Lily drawled as they left the orchard and headed back to Holly Springs. She tried not to feel disappointed she hadn't already lost her virginity.

"Believe me." Fletcher reached over and squeezed her hand. "You'll thank me later when you're ensconced in a nice comfortable bed." Keeping one hand on the wheel, he lifted her wrist to his lips, traced the inside of it with his lips and tongue. "Your place or mine?"

She thought of the twin canopy bed she had slept in since she had been a little girl. And for a lot of reasons never bothered to change. "I think you have the more comfortable bed," Lily allowed, aware, but not surprised at the way her heart was still pounding. After all, a big turning point in her life lay ahead...

"Good point." His mouth kicked up at the corner. He steered the truck over into a gravel turnaround alongside the road, shifted it into park and leaned across to kiss her again, hard. She leaned toward him and kissed him back. He reached down and released his safety belt, then hers. The next thing she knew she was being shifted across the bench-style seat and onto his lap. He brought her down across his hard-muscled thigh and the proof of his desire for her. The fiery intimacy of the contact robbed her of breath and left her shaken as the demanding feel of him scorched through her jeans. If this was what it was like now, she thought, as his mouth continued to mate with hers, his tongue stroking, tempting, tasting, heaven help her when they got to the really good stuff. She was about to melt from the inside out as it was...

And he was just as hot and bothered as she was, his skin burning through the fabric of his shirt and jeans with fiery intensity as he took full, masculine possession of her lips, then moved to her ear. One hand came up to cup her breast through the fabric of her T-shirt, while the other was unsnapping then unzipping her jeans. Lily moaned as his fingers slipped beneath the lacey edge of her thong panties to find her...there. The contact shot a jolt of exquisite pleasure through her, making her moan. She heard him chuckle as he began to kiss her again, and then she was being shifted off his lap again onto the cool leather seat of the cab. She stared over at him, aware her nipples had hardened into aching points, and lower still, there was a telltale dampness...and pulsing need.

The windows of the truck were fogged up. Her head felt the same way. She looked at him from a misty, pleasure-filled place. "Did I...?"

"No, no." He regarded her gently, looking struck by her innocence once again. "But you will several times before night's end, I promise.'' After reaching over to zip and snap her jeans, he refastened her seat belt then his. ''Right now—'' he looked determined as he checked to make sure the road was clear, then drove back out onto the country highway ''—we've got to concentrate on getting all the way home.''

''Good idea,'' Lily said, studying his handsome profile in the soft light of the dash. Because if they stopped one more time she sensed there would be no more holding back on either of their parts, no matter where they were....

''So.'' Fletcher's voice was gravelly with need as he searched for something nonarousing for them to talk about. ''What about Spartacus—?''

Somehow it seemed safer to close her eyes and let her head fall back against the padded headrest, than continue looking at the lips that had already given her so much pleasure. Lily drew in a shaky breath, aware she could barely think coherently. ''We don't have to walk him or anything. He's with your nephew, Christopher, for the evening.'' She licked her lips and tasted... Fletcher. ''I don't have to pick him up until tomorrow morning.''

''So we've got the whole night?''

Lily swallowed around the sudden, parched feeling in her throat. ''If you want it,'' she said shyly, knowing he was more than man enough for her. Was she woman enough for him?

''Oh, I want it,'' he said softly, reaching over to tangle his fingers in her hair. He teased her gently. ''Now if we could just hurry up and get there....''

Lily chuckled as he continued to drive safely nevertheless. "You really are in a hurry, aren't you?" The look on his face said he couldn't wait to start making love to her, really making love to her....

"To get started." He sent her a gentle, protective look as smug male confidence exuded from him in mesmerizing waves. "As for the rest, I plan to take my time."

And take his time he did. It was Lily who was in a hurry, who kept trying to speed things up. No sooner were they in the door to his apartment, than she was in his arms again, kissing him passionately, her desire for him fast outstripping everything else. Her fear about it being her first time...her wondering if it was going to hurt...seemed irrelevant. Lily cared only about the comforting feel of his arms around her, the enticing hardness of his body pressed up against hers and the blossoming love in her heart. She knew this was supposed to be just a casual fling—and maybe for him it was, she thought, as they continued to kiss each other hotly and possessively. But for her it was another step to a brand-new life filled with excitement and passion and the freedom to be and do whatever she wanted and needed. It was a life without restriction, and her body ignited as did her soul. This felt so right. Fletcher felt so right as he gave in to her urgency, swept her up into his powerful arms and carried her toward his bedroom, not setting her down until they had reached the side of the bed.

The covers were rumpled, as if he had just gotten out of them. He looked down at her, a pulse working in his throat, as Lily drank in the tantalizing fragrance of soap and man and the deliciously masculine cologne he favored. "If you want to opt out of this," he said, "now's the time."

Lily grinned. How like Fletcher to be the antithesis of the cynic he was publicly thought to be, and try and protect her, even now. "Not on your life," she said as she went up on tiptoe and kissed him yet again. Being here with Fletcher like this was her every fantasy come true. "And to show you," she murmured, taking the hem of her T-shirt and lifting it above her breasts, over her head. She flung it off and stood before him in a transparent wisp of a shell-pink demi-bra.

His chest rose and fell with each ragged breath. "Damn, Lily," he said as she reached around behind her, undid the clasp and let the bra slip off her arms.

His eyes darkened as he took in the silky curves of her breasts and jutting nipples. As their eyes met and the air between them reverberated with excitement and escalating desire, Lily felt more womanly than she had in her entire life.

"You are so beautiful."

"It's no wet T-shirt."

"Doesn't have to be." He took her hand and held it against the front of his jeans. "Can't you feel what you do to me?"

Lily smiled. So this was what it was like to be desired, to be wanted so very much you could hardly stand it.

"Your turn," she whispered playfully. He undid a button and then pulled the shirt over his head, flung it off and away from him.

For a moment, Lily could only stare. He was beautiful, too. More than beautiful. His shoulders were even broader than she had realized, his chest nicely muscled and satiny smooth. A mat of honey-brown hair spread across his chest and flat male nipples, before arrowing down to the waistband of his jeans. "Keep going," Lily said as she lounged against the bureau.

Holding her eyes, he reached for the buckle on his belt. "I thought it was ladies first," he teased, all too willing to strip for her if that was what she wanted. And it was...

"Not tonight." Lily smiled as he pulled off his boots, then dropped "trou," and without her even asking, divested himself of his dark gray boxer-briefs. His arousal was so pronounced, so velvety smooth, she couldn't tear her eyes away from it. "Damn, Fletcher," she murmured a little bashfully as he strode near.

"What are you thinking?" he asked as she continued to stare down at the visibly throbbing length.

"That there is no way that is ever going to fit inside of me."

He grinned. "Yes, it will. You'll see."

Lily brushed a hand across the taut skin of his abdomen. Paused. Licked her lips. "I don't know about that," she said shakily.

"Trust me. I do," Fletcher murmured back. He trailed his mouth over the tops of her breasts. Lily felt the hot moistness of his breath on her skin and a hot rush of desire swept through her. Her eyes drifted shut, even as she wondered how someone so big and strong and male could have such a tender touch. And then his lips were moving lower still, caressing the sensitive undersides of her breasts, the valley between, before settling on the sensitive tip. Her knees went weak as his mouth closed over her, drawing deep, and her body thrilled and burned with everything that had been missing for her. She moaned, arching up against him, tunneling her hands through his hair, holding him close even as she wanted more and more and more.

"You like that," he whispered as he replaced his lips with the pads of his thumbs and straightened to kiss her again, deeply, erotically, as if she were his and always would be....

"Oh yes," Lily whispered back. Making love with Fletcher was so much better than she had ever imagined it could be.

"Then let's keep going, shall we? 'Cause it's still your turn."

He stepped back. Lily had only to look into his eyes to know what he wanted her to do.

Mouth dry, she stepped out of her sandals. Unsnapped, then unzipped her jeans. She was trembling as she shoved them down her legs, stepped out of them. And stood before him clad only in the wispy pale pink thong. This time she didn't even have to ask. He liked what he saw. Very much.

She started to take it off, but he caught her hand and drew her down onto the bed. "Let me."

The next thing Lily knew she was lying on her back. Fletcher was once again parting her knees and lying between the cradle of her thighs. Her thong was still on. It didn't seem to bother him one bit as he kissed his way across the top edge of the fabric. Then he drifted lower, suckling gently. The friction of his lips and tongue through the barrier of lace was almost more than Lily could bear. She arched up off the bed. Her thighs fell even farther apart. Fletcher's free hand slid between them, stroking the tender insides from knee to pelvis and back down again. She was teetering on the edge of something wonderful…hot and melting inside…

"Fletcher," she moaned again, catching his head between her hands. He chuckled softly again, and this time her thong came off. And then his mouth was there, with nothing in between them, his fingers were parting the tender folds, sliding inside her. Making lazy circles, moving in, up, out again. Driving her crazy as more moisture flowed. And then something else was happening. She was trembling, aching, exploding inside until she quivered with pleasure and nearly shot all the way off the bed.

And Lily knew…finally…finally…

When she could, she lifted her head and found him stretched out beside her, smiling at her with a pleasure every bit as potent as her own. Lily caught her breath at the desire still etched on his handsome face. "That was it?"

His smile widened as he savored the way she continued to tremble and stroked her body playfully. "Let's call it a good start." He eased between her legs again, with a masculine resolve that had her surrendering to him all over again. "We've still got a ways to go."

Lily could see how much he cared, by the gentle restraint in his gaze. He was determined to make this as good for her as it was for him, first time or no. "How did I get so lucky?" she whispered around the sudden lump of emotion in her throat.

He draped a leg over hers and, still holding her as if he never wanted to let her go, still watching her face, let his fingers do their magic once again. "Beats me," Fletcher whispered back, his golden-brown eyes dark with a longing that seemed to go way beyond the sexual. "I've been asking myself the same question for days now," he whispered back meaningfully, his arousal pressing against her hip.

And then he was kissing her again, bringing her to the brink again, surprisingly quickly this time. Sheathing himself. Protecting them both. Shifting his strong hard body overtop of her. Kissing her full on the mouth until their bodies took up a primitive rhythm all their own, until their was no doubt how much they wanted their bodies to mesh. And then she was lifting her hips, pleading wordlessly for a more intimate union, and he was easing her knees apart, lifting her and parting her, pushing past that first fragile barrier to the welcoming warmth inside.

For a moment, Lily didn't think it was going to be possible. He was so big and so hard and so hot, and she was so tight. But as he rocked against her with gentle, patient insistence, she discovered their bodies were made for each other after all. And then they truly were one and the possessive look in his eyes made her catch her breath. Awash in sensation, Lily let her head fall all the way back, let the abandon overtake her. And then she was moaning again, whispering his name, urging him on as the remaining boundaries between them dissolved into a wild, sensual pleasure unlike anything she had ever known. And he, too, was soaring, pressing into her as deeply as he could go, and they were lost, free-falling into an ecstasy that warmed her body and filled her soul.

"I guess you were right," Lily said as they cuddled together afterward. She pressed her lips against his chest. "You did fit."

His laughter rumbled up inside his chest, a warm and welcoming sound. As he turned to face her, he looked proud to have been the one to claim her. "Who said dreams don't come true?" he murmured with a playful wink as he shifted her so she was beneath him, and began to make love to her all over again.

Indeed, Lily thought. Hers certainly had.

FLETCHER FELL ASLEEP with Lily snuggled against him, only to be rudely awakened by the phone ringing at 4:00 a.m. He groaned, reluctantly unwrapping his arms from around Lily's soft, incredibly warm and feminine body, and knocked the alarm clock off his nightstand while trying to get to the phone. "Fletcher Hart," he growled into the receiver as the metal clock continued to clatter against the hardwood floor before coming to a noisy halt that did little to stir the beautiful woman sleeping beside him. "And this damn well better be an emergency," he warned bad-temperedly.

"It's Dylan. And it is. I need a ride to the Raleigh-Durham airport."

Damn. Fletcher rubbed the sleep from his eyes. Wasn't it just his luck that the best night of his entire life would have to be so rudely interrupted? "When?" he growled in a way that let his younger brother know this better not become a habit. Now that Lily was his, Fletcher had plans for his nights.

"Now," Dylan said even more urgently. "My flight to Chicago departs at 6:05 a.m. and I'm supposed to be there two hours prior to departure to check-in. Obviously, I'm not going to make that," Dylan continued in his smooth TV sportscaster's voice. "But if we leave in the next ten, fifteen minutes I could probably make my flight."

Fletcher scowled as Lily finally began to stir. It felt as if he just went to sleep five minutes ago and yet all he wanted to do was make love to Lily all over again. Which might be possible if she woke all the way up...and wanted him, the way he now wanted her. "Any particular reason you called me?" he asked dryly. Instead of one of his other four brothers. All of whom lived in Holly Springs, too.

"We were all out until 2:00 a.m. and you went home early and I didn't think you'd be doing anything in particular right about now." Dylan paused meaningfully. "Are you?"

Just the most important thing in my entire life. "Besides sleeping?" Fletcher affected the most bored tone he could manage. "No. And what are you doing hopping on a plane to Chicago? Aren't you supposed to be here through the weekend given the fact our sister is getting married on Sunday?''

''Yeah, I know, I'm supposed to be on vacation until after the ceremony. But there's some kind of emergency at the TV station where I work and there's an all-hands-on deck meeting at the studio at noon today.'' Dylan's voice tensed even more. ''You know how volatile things can be.''

Fletcher did. The anchors and broadcasters were hired and fired all the time in that industry, often for very little reason save the station manager's whim. It wasn't an arena he would want to work in. But his sports-minded and hopelessly telegenic younger brother loved it.

''I figure I better be there,'' Dylan told Fletcher soberly.

''Gotcha,'' Fletcher said, knowing now why Dylan had called him. He was trying to save face and manage his fears, and Dylan figured Fletcher would be the least likely to pass judgment or advise him to get another career.

''But I'll be back in time for the wedding,'' Dylan promised matter-of-factly.

''Rehearsal?''

''That I can't say, but…''

''I understand,'' Fletcher said, knowing his brother was in an impossible situation. If he did go and ended up missing the wedding, the family would be ticked off at him. If he didn't go and lost his job as a result, he'd be screwed, as well. ''I'll be over to get you in a minute,'' Fletcher reassured him.

"Thanks. I'll be on the front steps at the Wedding Inn."

Another problem. "You didn't tell Mom you're leaving yet, did you?" Fletcher guessed and could practically see his brother's grimace in return.

"She'll find out soon enough when she reads the note I left for her on the kitchen table," Dylan said.

Shaking his head at his younger brother's cowardice—this kind of exit would *not* bode well with their mother—Fletcher hung up. Lily was propped on one elbow, watching him. She looked deliciously ravished. In need of proper loving again. And he had to leave. Damn.

"What's happening?" Lily asked as Fletcher stood and pulled on his jeans.

Briefly, Fletcher explained Dylan's predicament.

Lily got up and began to dress hurriedly, too. "Well, of course he has to go back to Chicago," she said.

Fletcher hoped his sister, Janey, felt that way. She might not. Brides were known to be irrational about their weddings, even women as normally cool, calm and collected as Janey. He had learned that growing up around the Wedding Inn. When it came to love, common sense often went right out the window.

"Besides," Lily continued as she bent over to slip on her sandals, "I need to get home soon, anyway. Lest our friends and neighbors see me departing at the crack of dawn and deduce I spent the night with you."

Fletcher didn't want Lily's reputation damaged any more than she did. He regretted having put her in this position and knew he should have thought about that before coaxing her to spend the entire night with him. Not that he was surprised by the lack of foresight on his part, he chided himself unhappily. If there was a mistake to be made, he usually made it. And larger than even this one was the bet he had made with Thad Lantz and his brothers, regarding Lily.

Lily looked at him curiously. "It'll be okay, Fletcher," she promised. "Really."

Would it? Fletcher wondered. Particularly if Lily ever found out what he had done....

Fletcher was still thinking about a way out of the mess he had created for himself when he dropped Lily at her home, pulled her to him and kissed her soundly. He might have inadvertently won his bet, but he could also lose everything that mattered to him. Particularly if word were to get out among the residents of Holly Springs. "We're going to have to talk about how to handle this. We can't have your reputation impugned."

Lily rolled her eyes at his concern. "After my too many margaritas incident and the bet I made—and lost—I don't think that's a consideration anymore," she drawled, before continuing even more recklessly. "And besides, wasn't that my purpose anyway? To reinvent myself in a wilder manner? So I would no longer be the prim-and-proper Lily or the Ice Princess of Holly Springs?"

She hadn't just slept with him for that reason. Had she? He asked himself.

"You helped me find my inner bad girl, Fletcher

Hart." Lily smiled and kissed him soundly once again as she slipped from the cab of his truck. "And for that I thank you."

WHEN LILY WENT OVER to Janey's to pick up Spartacus on her way to work later that morning, Spartacus leaped up from his spot near the front door and wagged his tail so hard he nearly fell over.

"He sure looks happy to see you!" Janey's son, Christopher, noted, moving a little stiffly as he ushered Lily inside the house. He was still recovering from an athletic injury, incurred over the summer, but otherwise looked good. His freckled cheeks glowed with healthy color, his blue eyes lively, his smile as friendly as could be.

Glad to see the gangly athlete doing so well, Lily knelt down to pet Spartacus and rub him behind his ears while he nuzzled her like a long-lost friend. "I'm happy to see Spartacus, too," Lily said and realized it was true.

"Are you going to adopt him?" Christopher asked, watching her expression carefully.

For the first time, the denials Lily had at the ready did not roll readily off her tongue. A dog, and the care he required, sort of conflicted with her new wild-and-free lifestyle. On the other hand, she was emotionally attached to the handsome yellow Lab.

"I don't know. I've never thought of myself as a dog person," Lily said finally as Spartacus stopped wagging and turned his soulful eyes up to hers. He seemed to know intuitively that Lily was thinking about finding him a home elsewhere.

"Well, if you decide you don't want him or can't keep him or whatever, let me know because I think I want him," Christopher said urgently.

"Christopher," Janey said as she walked in, "we talked about this. If you get a dog of your own, you need to have plenty of time to spend with him, especially at the beginning. And right now you still have physical therapy for your athletic injury last month, and school and homework and your part-time job at the arena. Honey, it's just not practical. And it wouldn't be fair to a dog like Spartacus who has already been through so much and needs so much tender loving care, just to feel safe and loved again."

Christopher nodded, understanding, but no less disappointed.

"Hey," Lily said, "tell you what. As long as I've got him, you can come over and see him and walk him anytime you want. He wasn't so good at first but he's getting pretty decent on a leash now. And you can even pet-sit him now as your schedule—and your mom—allow."

Christopher turned to Janey for permission.

Janey smiled. "Of course you can pet-sit Spartacus. In fact, I think it's a great idea for all concerned."

"Thanks, Mom." Christopher beamed. "And thank you, Ms. Madsen. You're awesome."

Lily grinned back. Maybe it was Fletcher, maybe it was just the fact she was finally getting over the loss of her grandmother, but she was beginning to feel really happy.

"Let me walk you out," Janey said. She and Lily

headed out onto Janey's front porch, Spartacus on a leash beside Lily. As they stood there together, Lily realized Janey and her son wouldn't be living there much longer. After the wedding, Janey and Christopher were set to move into Thad's much larger home. Being the practical woman she was, Janey had already put her home on the market. The Realtor's For Sale sign whipped around in the mounting wind as Janey cast a worried glance toward the darkening sky.

She looked back at Lily. "You're thinking what I'm thinking, aren't you?"

Lily nodded unhappily, guessing at the nature of her best friend's thoughts. "That this storm front heading into the area is going to put a damper on your outdoor wedding plans?"

Janey nodded. "If it rains for three days, there's no way we'll be able to have the ceremony in the formal gardens at the Wedding Inn. Even if we use tents, the ground will be a squishy mess. There'd be no walking on it, especially in heels."

"Thinking of moving it inside?" Lily asked, glad to see Janey was taking this in stride.

Janey nodded. "The chapel at Unity Church where we attend services is available for the ceremony, and we can use the Oak Room at the Wedding Inn for the reception. Although, if we do that, it's really going to mess up what we had planned in terms of flowers."

Lily knew what Janey meant. They had been planning to use the inn's lush garden hedges as an intricate part of many of the arrangements, draping garlands of flowers around the perimeter of the outdoor "chapel" where the ceremony and reception had been slated to take place.

"A wedding trellis woven with wildflowers just isn't going to look right inside the church," Janey worried. "Not with the stained-glass window overlooking the sanctuary."

"I agree. Tall sterling-silver candelabra would be better."

"And the Oak Room is so formal. But it's the room where we can seat two hundred for a wedding supper."

"I agree. Changing the site of the reception and the ceremony will require a complete redesign of all the flowers. You're probably going to want to go with something more in keeping with a traditional indoor wedding if you move it inside."

"But the flowers have already been ordered, haven't they?" Janey guessed, looking all the more worried.

Lily nodded. Janey had wanted to create a "sun-kissed meadow" effect for her Sunday-afternoon ceremony. She put a reassuring arm around Janey's waist. "I think we can still use all the flowers we ordered. We're just going to have to get more creative with how we arrange them."

"Oh, this is such a mess." Janey cast another look at the sky as big fat raindrops began to fall. "I so wanted my wedding to Thad to be perfect."

"And it will be," Lily promised with a smile, giving her friend's waist another squeeze. She didn't know if it was having Fletcher in her life, or the fact that she just felt so free to do what she pleased now, but suddenly she felt invincible. Like she could and would meet every challenge that came her way. "You just leave everything to me," she said.

"Thanks. I will. And speaking of you…"

"Yes?"

Janey cast a look over her shoulder to make sure her son was nowhere in sight. He was still inside, stuffing papers and books into a backpack. "What's going on between you and my brother?" Janey whispered.

"Fletcher?"

Janey rolled her eyes and quipped drolly, "That would be the one, all right."

Lily shrugged. The passion she felt for Fletcher was so new, she did not want to share it. "Nothing."

"Nothing, as in nothing really is going on?" Janey persisted in a voice barely above a whisper. "Or nothing, as in I'm really in love with him?"

Lily hesitated. She hadn't been aware she was wearing her heart on her sleeve. But since she was, maybe it was best she confide in someone. "It's that obvious?" she whispered back.

Janey nodded, her amber eyes serious.

"I've known him forever," Lily said. And she had always been attracted to him, even when he drove her crazy. "But we've never interacted the way we have lately," she finished shyly.

Janey reached over and squeezed Lily's hand. "Sometimes that's the way it happens. You just have to be in the right place at the right time with the right person."

It certainly felt as if that was the case all right, Lily thought, as Spartacus sat beside Lily patiently on the porch. Lily looked at Janey as the rain began to come down in earnest. Since they were talking, she could use some "sisterly" words of wisdom. "You got involved with Thad Lantz awfully fast." They'd begun seeing each other in July. Here it was August, and the two were getting married. "Do you have any qualms?"

"No," Janey said, and she looked so serene Lily knew it was true. "I feel like I've finally come home. It's funny, you know. For so many years, I felt I had to leave Holly Springs and live away from here to find my bliss. But it doesn't work that way. Your bliss isn't out there, somewhere else. It's right here—" Janey pointed to her heart "—inside. It was just up to me to find it. And now I know that true happiness is having a home and a child and a husband and being surrounded by family and friends. Doing work I care about, in a place I really adore is the icing on the cake. But I could do work I still loved a lot less and be happy, as long as I had Christopher and Thad and my mom and my brothers. And maybe, one day, even a dog. Although probably not until next summer," she finished wryly.

"You really do have it all," Lily said.

Janey leaned forward to give her a hug. "And someday you will, too," she promised.

Lily hoped that was the case. Finally, it seemed, she had found a man she loved. A man who had the potential to make her really, truly happy, not just for the immediate present, but for the rest of her life. The question was, how did Fletcher Hart feel about her?

"YOU'LL NEVER GUESS what I just heard!" Sheila told Lily and Maryellen breathlessly as she returned from her lunch break.

"Action?" Maryellen teased.

Lily smiled. Like almost everyone else in Holly Springs, her three part-time employees couldn't seem to resist going over to gawk at the TV production being filmed in the historic downtown area. Not that there was much to hear. They were kept well back from any dialogue being spoken and had to content themselves with watching—from a distance—the individual scenes being filmed.

"No. Custom Florists from Raleigh just got fired from their set-decorating job."

Belinda settled on a stool and rested a hand on the baby growing inside her. "You're kidding. Their work is spectacular."

"I know, but that burgundy-haired girl—you know, the one that wears all the eyeliner..."

"Carson McRue's assistant."

"Right." Sheila nodded vigorously as she slipped off her rain jacket and hung it on a hook by the door. "She came over and told them they had to leave. They weren't going to be decorating the church for the wedding scene."

"Maybe they're just delaying the filming because of the rain."

Lily knew not much had been going on that day thus far because of the heavy downpours.

"That's what Custom Florists hoped," Sheila continued as she put her umbrella out to dry. "But it's not the case. Carson's assistant told them not to come back tomorrow, either. Carson McRue Productions would send them a check for any time spent thus far, but they weren't going to be needed after all."

Lily shrugged, refusing to get excited. "It's possible the set decorators are going to do it themselves. This weather delay has to have cost them a pretty penny. So maybe they're just trying to make it up that way."

"Carson McRue doesn't come across like a man who pinches pennies," Belinda said.

"Don't look now, but here comes the assistant," Maryellen murmured.

And right behind her was Fletcher Hart. He held the door for the assistant, waiting while she closed her umbrella, then marched toward Lily purposefully. The assistant spoke first. "Ms. Madsen? Carson wants to see you over in his trailer."

"About…?" Lily asked while her staff glanced at her hopefully. Lily was trying to keep her mind on business, but it was difficult—to say the least—with Fletcher standing there in a long yellow rain slicker and hat looking as sexy and indomitable as any cowboy who had ever come in out of a storm.

While Fletcher took off his hat and ran his fingers through his rain-dampened hair, his amber eyes giving off a welcoming glint, the assistant popped her gum and ran her index finger across one heavily made-up eye. "Um, officially, I think he wants you to decorate the church or something," she said.

Lily paused as Fletcher leaned a shoulder against the wall and regarded her with the same intensity he had used when making love to her over and over again.

Feeling herself go weak in the knees, just contemplating what had happened the previous night and what she hoped would happen again very soon, Lily turned her attention back to the conversation at hand. She wasn't averse to new business, celebrity or otherwise, but she had previous obligations that had to be met first. "When?" she asked, wishing Fletcher would stop looking at her as if he were thinking about kissing her again. It was making it impossible for her to concentrate.

"Whenever the rain stops and they can continue with the filming," the assistant said.

It wasn't supposed to cease for at least another day. Lily noted Fletcher was not looking happy about the request. "And unofficially?" Lily asked Carson's assistant.

She popped her gum again. "Carson's bored, waiting out this rain, and he'd like someone to while away the time with, as per usual."

Not good, Lily thought as Fletcher lifted a coolly discerning brow. "Why me?" Lily asked as Fletcher's scowl deepened. *He was behaving as protectively as her grandmother had when she was alive.* Lily didn't like it. His coming to her rescue last night had been one thing. His obvious skepticism of her ability to make a proper judgment about a business decision was another.

Doing her best to conceal her hurt that Fletcher

had as little faith in her as her grandmother ultimately had, Lily turned her glance back to Carson's messenger.

The assistant shrugged. "You're young, blond, pretty, got that whole innocent angel thing going for you. It's exactly his type, when he's on location anyway."

And what was Fletcher's type? Lily wondered as she briefly sought his glance once again. At the moment it did not seem to be anyone as independent-minded as she was. Under normal circumstances, anyway.

Across the square, the door to Carson's trailer opened. His costar for that episode stormed out, moving hurriedly across the blocked off area. She did not look happy.

It wasn't too hard to figure out what was going on. Able to feel her employees hovering around her like concerned mother hens, Lily smiled at the assistant. Two days ago she would have jumped at the chance to spend time alone with Carson McRue, even if she spent that time fending off amorous advances. Not now. She had all the passion and excitement she needed in her life with one Fletcher Hart.

"I don't think so," Lily replied without an ounce of regret. "Thanks for asking, but we're all working pretty hard on the flowers for the Hart-Lantz wedding."

The assistant muttered something indecipherable. "Carson isn't going to like this," she warned.

Lily kept working on the arrangement in front of her, one of dozens of summer bouquets that were going to be placed around the church and in the Oak Room at the Wedding Inn. Ignoring the masculine possessiveness radiating from Fletcher, she said, "Not my problem."

The assistant sighed as she exited the shop, re-opening her umbrella as soon as she cleared the door. "Don't we wish we could both say that," she said over her shoulder.

As soon as she left, Fletcher came toward Lily. He looked relieved she had turned down both the work and the chance to spend time alone with the TV star. "I'm meeting my brother Joe at Crabtree Mall in Raleigh to do a wedding errand. We're going to have lunch while we're there. You want to go?"

Lily was tempted, despite her unexpressed pique with Fletcher. "I wish I could," she said wistfully, feeling suddenly unbearably restless. Unable to help but note how handsome he looked standing there, hat in hand, with the rain dotting his thick hair, she continued softly. "But we've got way too much to do here to get ready for Janey's wedding." And she needed time to think. To figure out how to handle this relationship if that was indeed what it was going to be, and not just the brief, passion-and-fun-filled fling she had initially signed on for.

"A rain check then," Fletcher answered oblivious to the interested looks emanating from Lily's employees.

Lily nodded her assent. And when they did talk alone again, she was going to have to counsel him on what rights—if any—being her lover entailed. Because there was no way she was going back to a life of being told what and what not to do, in business or her private life. Even if she was head over heels in love with him.

"DYLAN SEEMS TO THINK we all owe you a hundred bucks," Joe told Fletcher lazily as they walked into Crabtree Mall to pick up the wedding rings for Thad and Janey.

"Yeah?" Fletcher pretended he had nothing to hide. "Where did Dylan get that idea?"

"The smile on your face when you picked him up this morning."

Fletcher shoved aside his guilt about a promise that was surely broken. "I smile all the time," he told his hockey-playing younger brother.

"Not when you're hauled out of bed at 4:00 a.m., you don't." Joe regarded Fletcher closely. "Seriously, what's up with you and Lily Madsen? Are you just chasing her to win this bet you made with all of us?"

To Fletcher's irritation Joe seemed to think that could indeed be the case. "The bet has nothing to do with my getting her out of that club last night," Fletcher bit out.

Joe remained unconvinced as they strolled past a popular clothing chain. "Then what does?"

"I was just looking out for her."

"Does Lily know that's all it was?"

"Lily knows the score." *That she's my woman now and will be from this point forward.*

Joe swore roundly, shook his head. "From where

I was standing it looked like Lily was reading a lot more into it than that.''

Good, Fletcher thought. Because he was, too.

''If she ever finds out about the bet—'' Joe continued, prophesizing grimly.

Fletcher cut Joe off. ''She'd never understand. Which is why I'm not going to tell her. And none of you is, either.'' Maybe in time, when he and Lily were close enough, when she trusted him enough to understand he had never—would never—hurt her, Fletcher would be able to tell Lily everything. About the promise to her grandmother, as well as the bet. Right now that was hardly a foregone conclusion on Lily's part. Particularly since she seemed to be treating their relationship like an exciting fling—nothing more, nothing less.

''Well, I hope you know what you're doing,'' Joe said worriedly as the beeper at Fletcher's waist buzzed.

Fletcher frowned as he unclipped the electronic device from his belt and saw who was calling.

''Clinic?'' Joe asked.

Fletcher shook his head. ''Carson McRue Productions.''

Chapter Nine

Fletcher surveyed the beautiful young stallion being unloaded from the horse trailer in the middle of the town square. There had been a break in the rain that had inundated them for two days, but the streets were wet, the gutters full of pooling water, and it looked as if it could start up again at any moment. The gray weather perfectly matched his unpleasant mood.

"There's no way I'm signing off on this," Fletcher told Carson McRue as the stallion Carson had personally selected to be in his show snorted and pranced about nervously.

"I think you misunderstand your role," Carson McRue said as out of his peripheral vision Fletcher saw Lily step out of Carson McRue's trailer, multi-colored papers in hand. She was followed by Carson's burgundy-haired assistant. What the hell…?

"You don't call the shots here," Carson continued haughtily. "We do. You, Dr. Hart, are a figurehead or paper-pusher at best."

Trying not to think what Lily had been doing in the arrogant actor's trailer, Fletcher turned his attention back to the important argument at hand. The temperamental horse was tossing his head and straining against the lead as his trainer attempted unsuccessfully to get the animal saddled up. "Yeah? Well, I'm not too ineffective to misunderstand the basic safety issues involved in using that horse. I know that animal. I've worked on him. He's far from trained. There's no way you can put him in a crowd situation, never mind expect there's a chance he'll do what is expected of him while you are filming."

"Why don't you leave that to me?"

"I would," Fletcher shot back angrily, "if I hadn't been hired to oversee the treatment of animals on this set."

"Well, fortunately that's something that can be easily fixed. You're fired."

Fletcher blinked. "What?"

"You heard me." Carson McRue signaled to one of the uniformed production security men who was standing guard around the perimeter of the barricaded area.

"Dr. Hart is no longer to be given access to the set."

The burly guard reached for Fletcher. Fletcher held him off with an upraised palm. "I'm leaving," he told the guard. To Carson, he said, "You're making a mistake."

"Mine to make," Carson retorted, smooth as silk. Turning away from Fletcher, he lifted his hand expansively. "Lily. Get all the papers signed?"

What papers? Fletcher wondered as Lily neared them. Her cheeks were flushed, whether with guilt or awareness of Carson's TV star status, Fletcher couldn't tell. "Yes, I did," Lily told Carson in a crisp professional tone.

"I'll see you first thing in the morning then— 6:00 a.m. Unity Church?"

"I'll be there," Lily promised. Refusing to make eye contact with Fletcher, she gave Carson a brief smile and hurried away.

Carson gave Fletcher a look of triumph, then headed off to the still-bucking and snorting horse.

Fletcher strode after Lily and followed her down Main Street and into Madsen's Flower Shoppe. "What was that about?" he asked. Outside it began to rain in torrents once again.

Lily set the papers on the counter and didn't answer right away.

"Tell me," Fletcher said, his heart sinking like a stone, "you have not just agreed to work for Carson McRue."

Lily's moment of feeling good for her unasked-for coup d'état faded as quickly as it had come. Aware that Sheila, Belinda, Maryellen and even Spartacus— who was curled up on his cushion behind the counter chewing a rawhide—were all watching her with wide-eyed amazement, Lily motioned Fletcher into her private office. "Let's take this in there," she said.

Chin high, she led the way. Fletcher followed.

Lily shut the door behind them, noting his whole body was taut with tension. "I'm sorry you got fired."

"Not as sorry as Carson McRue and his production are going to be when that horse wrecks everything—and possibly everyone—in sight.''

Lily paused, her stomach fluttering nervously. ''You really think someone will get hurt?'' she asked quietly.

Fletcher nodded grimly. Worry darkened his eyes. ''Yes, I do. He needs a stunt horse that is used to following directions and working around cameras.''

Her own problems forgotten, Lily searched for a solution. ''Can't you appeal to someone?''

''Who? McRue owns the production company. It's the production company that's liable.''

''Maybe it will be okay,'' Lily said, sitting down on the edge of her desk.

For a long moment, Fletcher remained motionless. He looked unconvinced. Then he abruptly gave it up and sauntered closer.

''You haven't explained what you were doing in Carson's trailer.''

She tilted her head at him, wondering what kind of rights he thought their intimacy of the night before gave him. ''Do I owe you an explanation?''

Fletcher paused. He seemed to think so, but stubbornly refused to admit as much. ''It's a job, Fletcher,'' Lily told him, her exasperation mounting as she moved away from the desk, and away from him.

''Right.'' He sent her a glance that told her he didn't intend to jump through any hoops for her. ''And I'm the tooth fairy.''

Lily whirled to face him and planted her hands on

her hips. "Exactly what are you accusing me of here?"

His glance drifted over her pastel T-shirt and trim khakis before returning ever so slowly to her eyes. He lounged back against the opposite wall, one booted foot across the other, his body at an angle. His eyes glinted with a mixture of doubt and cynicism that stung. "You wanted to date him," he reminded her softly. "That date was circumvented."

"By you," Lily reminded, not about to let Fletcher get the upper hand or begin to think he had the right to tell her what she could and could not do. She was no longer in a place where she would allow herself to be reined in.

"Do you still want to date him?" Fletcher asked.

Lily stared at Fletcher in confusion. *I thought I was dating you. I thought that was what us making love meant.* Had she been wrong? Had it been just a one-night stand and she was too naive, too inexperienced, to know that? All Lily knew was that she couldn't discuss it here. Couldn't bear to find out here and now she had been wrong about Fletcher's intentions toward her. She didn't want to know she had been just a pleasant albeit different diversion for him.

He shoved a hand through his hair. "Listen, Lily, I know you don't want to hear it, but you can't handle him."

And she'd thought her days of being coddled and treated like an infant were over. "What I can't handle is you!" Lily said, starting for the door.

Fletcher moved to block her way. He gave her a

self-assured, faintly baiting look. "The guy wants to go to bed with you."

Lily tossed her head. "You are so cynical!"

He closed in on her deliberately, not stopping until there was a scant two inches between them. He looked very grim. Disapproving, almost. "I'm right!"

Lily threw up her hands in frustration, refusing to back away, even though being this close to him made her heart pound and her body tingle all over. "You always think things are going to turn out badly and expect the worst of everyone."

"At least I'm realistic," Fletcher countered just as determinedly. A hint of the old cynicism flashed in his eyes. "Not going through life in a protective bubble. Blaming everyone else for your innocence, when really it's your inability to wise up and see the world as it really is instead of the way you wish it was!"

"Okay. That's it!" Lily grabbed him by the shoulders and shoved him toward the door.

On the other side, Spartacus let out a short, warning bark, then a low, fierce growl.

"Out of here!" Lily commanded Fletcher.

Fletcher went, albeit not willingly, through the storeroom where the worktables and big refrigerators were kept toward the back door. As she opened the alley door, he started to say something else. Probably another warning. Lily's temper kicked into full gear and she cut him off with a look.

"You're right—I don't want to hear it!" Lily snapped and slammed the door after him.

"AND SO the miserable rain continues," Lily told Spartacus hours later as she tore down yet another heavy velvet drapery and added it to the heap on the wide plank pine floors. It was dark outside, but she had left one plantation shutter open so Spartacus could see the street outside. And it was as she turned her glance that way that Spartacus let out a low warning growl. Lily saw the shadow of a man with familiar kick-butt posture moving across the porch. Then the doorbell rang.

Her heart racing in anticipation, she went to get it with Spartacus trotting at her side. Fletcher was standing on the other side of the threshold. Raindrops glistened in his hair and dotted his starched long-sleeved navy blue shirt, jeans and the toes of his custom boots. He had a bouquet of flowers in one hand and a box of candy, a CD and a DVD in the other. He held them out. Her eyes locked with his, she accepted them wordlessly and felt her heartbeat kick up yet another notch as their fingers brushed. Damn him, she thought, for making her want him all over again.

Knowing if she didn't stop looking into his beautiful amber eyes she would end up in his arms, kissing him again as if there was no tomorrow, she dropped her gaze to the gifts he had brought. Closer inspection showed the DVD to be an old Disney favorite Lily recalled watching with her grandmother when she was a kid. *"Pollyanna?"* she remarked dryly.

A smile tugged at the corner of his lips. "I thought

we could watch it together and you could help me learn how not to be so cynical.''

"And the music?" Ignoring the butterflies jumping around in her stomach, she pointed to the soundtrack for *Love Affair*.

He shrugged his broad shoulders affably and leaned his shoulder against the portal. "Figured it sort of fit the mood since that was what we were in. The flowers were on your list of things you wanted to experience. And Janey may have mentioned to me you have a fondness for gourmet chocolates.''

Despite her earlier decision to stay angry with him just this side of forever, she was impressed. And she wondered what it all meant. "You went all out here," Lily noted cautiously.

Their gazes meshed, held. "I wasn't taking any chances," Fletcher told her softly, all the love she had ever wanted to see in his eyes. "I wanted you to let me in the door so I could tell you just how sorry I was for behaving like a jealous fool today.''

Just that swiftly, her anger with him evaporated and the last of her pride disappeared. "Come in." She motioned him across the threshold and went to put her gifts down. She still didn't know where their relationship was headed or if they even had a relationship. All she was certain of was that she was very glad to see him.

Spartacus, however, was not so quick to forgive. He was still on his cushion in front of the window, but he had stopped chewing on his rawhide and was watching Fletcher with dark cautious eyes.

Fletcher seemed to know an apology was called

for there, too. He hunkered down beside Spartacus and offered his hand, palm up. "Sorry I scared you this afternoon, buddy," he said. "I was just going all protective on my woman here."

My woman. Lily thrilled at the words.

Fletcher rubbed Spartacus behind his ears. "One of these days you're going to fall for some good-looking female and all you're going to want to do is keep her safe, too. But what you've got to realize is that the really strong and feisty ones like Lily here can protect themselves." Fletcher paused and looked at Lily meaningfully. "They don't need us to step in and do it for them."

"Amen to that," Lily said quietly as her world righted once again.

Fletcher stood, took Lily into his arms. "I know you felt smothered sometimes, growing up," he told her as he smoothed a hand through her hair. "I'm sorry if I did the same thing to you."

Lily accepted his apology as their eyes meshed. "Just don't do it again," she cautioned softly.

"Yes, ma'am." Fletcher tipped an imaginary hat at her.

Lily broke into a grin while Spartacus regarded Fletcher for another long, assessing moment. Deciding he could trust Fletcher again, Spartacus wagged his tail once tentatively, then more eagerly. Fletcher patted the Lab on the head, then gestured at the sketch pads strewn across the coffee table, and the draperies heaped in piles on the floor. "What's going on here?" Fletcher asked Lily.

Lily shrugged, a little embarrassed by the mess. "I

was working on the plans for Janey's wedding. You know we're moving the ceremony indoors?''

Fletcher nodded. ''Mom said something about it when I talked to her earlier.''

''So we're having to reconfigure all the floral arrangements, some of which we went ahead and did today and put in the refrigerators at the shop. I think I've finally got it all worked out although I want to go over the revised plans with Janey tomorrow just to be sure.'' It was important Janey be happy with the finished product.

Fletcher's gaze went back to the velvet heaped on the floor. ''You're taking down the drapes for cleaning?''

Lily shook her head. ''I'm getting rid of them,'' she said firmly. ''If I'm going to stay here, it's time I made this place my own.''

Fletcher had to admit it opened the place up, getting rid of all the heavy velvet drapery. She'd also removed the doilies from the tables, rolled up the ancient rug with the cabbage patch roses and taken a couple of not particularly interesting paintings from the wall. It had left white marks on the yellowed floral wallpaper of the front parlor.

''What are you going to do in here?'' Fletcher asked, pleased to see Lily taking charge of her life.

''Strip the walls, paint them creamy white and put two comfortable sofas in here in a neutral hue. Probably put down a gorgeous fire-engine-red Persian rug and use accessories to tie it all together. I want to bring this place into the twenty-first century.''

Fletcher envisioned the new décor. "I think Rose would approve."

Lily met his smile shyly. "I think she would, too."

The companionable feeling between them deepened. Fletcher edged nearer. "What are you going to do with the rest of the stuff?"

"I've contacted several antiques dealers. They're coming in to appraise the belongings of the house. I'm going to sell all but the most basic pieces and use the proceeds to finance the refurbishing."

He sent her an admiring glance, pleased at the strides she was making. "You really are moving on."

Already, she didn't seem to need him the way she had just a few days ago. And although he was relieved to see it, the change worried him, too. He had started to like the way she turned to him for comfort and advice. Not to mention the distinctly male satisfaction he derived whenever he charged to her rescue. For the first time, he saw himself as half of a couple. And although that was alarming—it was a lot easier not to get emotionally or romantically involved—it was also a sign that he was growing up, too.

Lily raked her teeth across her soft lower lip and turned her gaze up to his. "You started me thinking the other night. I realized a couple of things. I love Madsen's Flower Shoppe. I love being a florist. It's what I would have done regardless." An affectionate glimmer crept into her eyes. "And I love this house. The reason I felt trapped was that I never took either over and made it my own. I never tried to create a life for myself different from the one Grandmother Rose envisioned for me.''

"But you're ready to do that now," Fletcher ascertained, not sure why the possibility of that should worry him so.

"Oh, yes," Lily said. She closed the distance between them and wreathed both slender arms about his neck. "And I know *exactly* how I want to start."

Chapter Ten

Lily had never been the aggressor. But if she wanted to leave her reputation behind, she knew she had to start going after what she wanted, and she couldn't think of a better place to do that than right here, right now. She rose on tiptoe, tangled her fingers in his hair and kissed him deeply. Responding passionately, he plundered her mouth, wrapped his arms around her and brought her close. She trembled in his arms and then his lips were on her throat, the lobe of her ear, the soft hollow beneath.

"Much more of this," Fletcher whispered, his warm breath teasing her ear, "and I'm going to want to take you upstairs."

Lily smiled and drew back so he could see the hunger on her face. "Then that makes two of us," she told him softly, tucking her hand in his, "because I want to go upstairs, too."

Leaving Spartacus curled contentedly up by the front windows, still chewing on a rawhide and watching the occasional car go by, Lily and Fletcher walked up the massive walnut staircase that dominated the foyer. Not content to let her call all the shots, he stopped to kiss her on the landing and then again at the top of the stairs. Shivers danced along her skin, from every point of contact, every tender caress. Emotions soaring, Lily kissed him back, enjoying the feel of him against her—and the knowledge that soon they would be together again in the most intimate way a man and woman could be. Blood rushing hot and needy through their veins, they continued kissing their way down the hall. But instead of going all the way to Lily's bedroom, Lily stopped him at the master bedroom suite.

Fletcher's eyes widened. Lily knew what he was thinking. It looked like a tornado had hit in there, too. She had rolled up the rugs, torn down the heavy brocade draperies that had hung on the bed and covered the row of windows that fronted the street and taken down all the ancient knickknacks and doilies and heaped them into boxes. She'd had new linens delivered to the store that day, which she had promptly brought home and put on the bed. They went well with the white plantation shutters still on the windows. Two scented candles stood sentry on the twin nightstands. There was a fresh bouquet of lilacs on the bureau, another on her old-fashioned mirrored dressing table.

"Wow," Fletcher said, still looking around.

Lily brought their clasped hands together and rested her cheek against the back of his wrist. "About time I abandoned my childhood bed and moved into the grown-ups' quarters, wouldn't you say?" She turned his hand over and pressed a kiss into the callused warmth of his palm.

Fletcher nodded, even as a hint of some uniden-
tified emotion—guilt maybe—flashed across his
handsome face. And just as suddenly, Lily felt
Fletcher pull away from her emotionally once again.

Lily sat down on the edge of the bed. She toed off
her sandals and ran her toes across the bare wood
floor. Fletcher was still standing there, looking as if
he'd just had a major attack of conscience. Which
again made her wonder: What was this relationship
of theirs? Where was it really going? He'd just now
said they were lovers, that he wanted to see things
her way.

Maybe it was time she saw things from his per-
spective, too. "Are you sorry for deflowering the florist?" she quipped. Was it her previous virginity that
was suddenly at issue here? Was that making him
feel beholden to her in some way he didn't really
want?

He locked gazes with her and sauntered closer,
abruptly looking as relaxed about what was happening between them as she was. "No. Oddly enough,
I'm not," he told her tenderly. "Although—" the
corners of the mouth that had given her such unbelievable pleasure quirked up in a self-deprecating
smile "—the gentlemanly part of me—the part of
me that was reared by Helen Hart—thinks I probably
should be full of remorse."

"But you're not," Lily ascertained happily.

He sat beside her on the bed. "No. I'm not. I'm
happy that I was your first—your only—lover. The
question is," Fletcher said, his eyes darkening ar-

dently, "how do you feel about being robbed of your innocence by me?"

Lily knew a lot was riding on her answer. "Truthfully?"

He nodded soberly, looking deep into her eyes.

"Happy." Lily swallowed around the sudden parched feeling in her throat. "And content in a way I've never been before." She couldn't explain it. She just knew whenever she was with Fletcher like this, she felt safe. Cherished. Protected. In a way she never had before, and never would again....

"Good. Me, too," Fletcher said then he took his time kissing her again. "Now all we have to do," he teased her lightly, already unbuttoning his shirt, "is figure out how we're going to go about making everything else on that wish list of yours come true."

Lily blushed hotly. There was no doubt at all in her mind what he was referring to now.

"I thought you wanted to speak up for yourself, access that inner bad girl and be the sexy woman you know you could be," he teased.

It was all Lily could do not to groan out loud. Pretending a great deal more insouciance than she felt, she stretched out sideways on the bed and propped her head on her upraised hand. "So here's my chance?" she replied playfully. "Is that what you're telling me?"

His eyes held the keys to thousands of erotic fantasies. He waggled his brows at her suggestively.

As the silence drew out between them, she realized he really expected her to confess her secret sexual fantasies to him. A self-conscious heat filling her from head to toe, she turned away from that knowing gaze. Moaning and falling back on the bed, she threw her arm across her face to further shade her feelings.

Smelling nicely of aftershave, mint-flavored toothpaste and soap, he sprawled next to her, looking ready to wait her out until dawn if necessary. He leaned over to kiss her shoulder. "It's not really that hard, Lily."

Lily moaned again, even more loudly. "Says the experienced one."

He plucked the forearm from her eyes and placed it above her head. He traced the uppermost curve of her breasts with his fingertip. "I'm not as experienced as you might think. Except in my fantasies." The wicked gleam was back in his amber eyes as he confessed huskily, "*There* I think I've probably earned a few awards."

She perked up a little at the thought she wasn't the only one capable of daydreaming. A lot. "Yeah? Really?"

He nodded.

Lily thought about that. "What are your fantasies?" she asked curiously.

Fletcher slid a hand beneath her T-shirt and lightly caressed her abdomen, before sliding up over her ribs to her breasts. Making an L of his index finger and thumb, he brought his hand up over her lace-covered breasts, down again, then up, rubbing her nipples into aching points. "I thought we were doing yours." He leaned over to first reveal and then kiss her navel.

Telling herself there would be plenty of time to reach fulfillment later, Lily lifted his hand and set it beside her. "We're getting to that." She sat up and faced him, cross-legged, on the bed. "You first."

He lay back lazily, arms folded behind him. The cynical smile that had always been so much a part of him was back. "You really want to hear this," he said.

Lily nodded earnestly. Maybe this didn't have to be such a one-way street. Maybe she could make his dreams come true, too.

"Well, since you brought it up, I always wanted my lover to do a striptease just for me."

Lily felt as if she had just won the lottery. She slapped her knee. "You're kidding. That's one of mine!" she said excitedly.

Fletcher lifted a disbelieving brow. "You wanted your lover to strip for you?"

"Well, sure. After I stripped for him, of course."

He sat up slowly and eyed her cautiously, the hint of a very naughty smile tugging at the corners of his lips. "Well? What do you say? Are you up for it?"

Lily bit her lip. He was really going to do this. "We don't have any stripper music," she said.

His grin widened to a voltage that melted her insides. "I bet you've got something that's sort of sexy," he encouraged her. "You being a person with an inner bad girl and all."

Lily paused. Part of her wanted to run and hide. The other part of her wanted to see this through to the exciting end. Just as she knew the chance to be this playful, this adventurous might not ever come again. And hadn't she waited a lifetime to break free of the many constraints around her?

"Ahhh. You're weakening. I can see it," Fletcher teased.

No way was he going to be able to call her chicken. "You wait here," Lily directed with a toss of her head. "I'll be right back."

Fletcher lay back on the bed and closed his eyes while Lily sashayed on out of the bedroom and down the hall to the childhood bedroom where most of her belongings were still stored.

A few seconds later, he heard the music floating down the hall. Interesting choice, he thought, as he lay there listening to the defiantly sultry voice of a popular rock star. And even more interesting attire.

Lily had shed the khakis and pastel T-shirt she'd been wearing when he arrived and was standing there in a getup that could only have come from one of the more risqué lingerie places at the mall. Curves that were almost too sinful to be borne were spilling out of a red lace bustier, matching garter and thong. Thigh-high stockings and high heels that made the most of her spectacular legs completed the drop-dead sexy look. She had a silk scarf in her hands and was dancing to the song "Fever." Proving, Fletcher noted as his lower half suffused with heat, she had all the moves required to stop a man's heart.

Mouth dry, he watched as she sashayed closer, never losing the beat. She grinned at the look on his face. Gripping the ends of the scarf with both hands, she pirouetted closer, giving him maximum view of the curves spilling out of her décolleté.

Deciding to enjoy the show, he stayed right where

he was. Let out a low wolf whistle. "Wow," he said
again in thoroughly male appreciation, urging her on.

Eyes gleaming seductively, she climbed up beside
him on the high four-poster bed, and careful of the
heels she was still wearing, moved to straddle his
torso. Taking one arm from behind his head, she
brought it toward her, then got the other. Wrapped
both wrists in silk, binding them together.

Fletcher lifted a brow, wondering what she was up
to now. "You said it was my choice," she reminded
playfully.

"And a fascinating choice it is," he agreed as she
lifted his wrists, and still straddling him, secured his
wrists to the post on that side of the headboard. Finished, she stayed right where she was. Expression
intent, she reached down and began unbuttoning his
shirt, starting at the top and working her way down.

"I thought you were the one going to be doing
the disrobing," he murmured.

She leaned over to reveal the surprisingly ample
swells of her breasts. "Don't you like the view?"

"Oh, I like." He caught his breath as she
smoothed her hands over his chest, eliciting sparks
of fire every place she touched, and wondered where
his trademark cynicism had gone. Because now it
was Fletcher who felt as if he'd never experienced
such sexual intimacy before. "It's just—" he
groaned as she found his belt and worked her magic
on that, too "—I don't want to get ahead of you."
And at the rate they were going, he was going to hit
the finish line before she even entered the race.

She sent him a wickedly provocative look as his

heart hammered in his chest, all angel and innocence again. "Why don't you let me worry about that?" she whispered seductively. Looking intent on what she was doing, she unzipped his fly, slid her hands inside. By the time she actually cupped him in her palm, he was throbbing with the need to possess her.

Grimacing with the effort to control his building desire, he reached up to try and free himself.

She caught his fingers before he could reach the knot. "You'll have your turn later."

"Promise?"

She whispered a sigh of pure pleasure. "Oh, yeah."

Their eyes locked. Agreement made, she moved back down his body, stripping off his boots, socks and pants as she went. The shirt was obviously going to have to stay on, they realized at once. She couldn't get it off unless she untied him, and the decidedly mischievous look on her face said she obviously had no intention of untying him. Who would have thought that she'd be such a vixen...?

She smoothed her hands over the muscles of his thighs, slipped them beneath him to trace the small of his back and the curve of his buttocks, before moving forward again to the most sensitive part of him. "Kiss me," he murmured, promising himself that when it was his turn, he was going to repeat the sweet torture, and then some.

"All right." She slid lower and put her mouth on him.

That hadn't been what Fletcher had meant. But it felt so damn good all he could do was close his eyes and groan. Lost in the feel of her moving so sweetly and patiently across him, taking possession, claiming him as her own. Just as he wanted to claim her. "Lily—" He caught his breath again.

"Right." He was pretty sure she deliberately misunderstood as she moved away from him and got back off the bed. "Time for the floor show, hmm, Fletch?"

Proving all over again how adept she was at moving to the beat, she moved her body sinuously, capturing his complete attention before slowly reaching behind her to unclasp her bustier. It took forever before her breasts spilled free, but seeing that creamy flesh and apricot nipples as the lace fell away from her silky skin brought forth a pleasure of another kind. Ditto each individual high-heeled shoe and stocking, the garter belt and finally the tiny triangle of string and lace. By the time she had bared herself to him and climbed back on the bed, Fletcher felt he had been wanting her his entire life. And maybe he had been, he thought as she climbed astride him, slipped a condom on him, because she looked like she had been waiting for him, too. "Untie me," he rasped, eager to take her the way she was meant to be taken—utterly and completely.

Lily grinned, all bad girl now. "No." With another wickedly playful grin, she bent over him, her breasts teasing his chest, her thighs cupping the outside of his. Holding his face between her hands, she kissed him. It was…magic.

"Stubborn," Fletcher murmured against her mouth, and then all rational thought was lost as she fused their mouths deeply and completely and opened her body to his. Hot, wet silk. Fevered kisses. Soft, warm breasts. She was everything he had ever wanted in a woman, and more. As she flattened her torso over his, he lost himself in the ecstasy of making love to her, putting everything he had into the joining. He waited until she soared to shattering erotic heights before he finally let go, too.

For long moments afterward they lay together, breathing hard, her face buried in his neck. Enjoying the pleasure of feeling her close, he kept his eyes shut, letting the aftershocks flow through them. Until aching desire surged through him once again. Damned if he didn't want to hold her close. ''Lily.'' The word came out half warning, half-frustrated moan.

''I know.'' She laughed softly and reached up to undo the knot. As soon as he was free, he caught her with both hands and brought her back down on the sheets beside him. ''You're a very bad girl,'' he told her as he stretched out over her, his body already hardening once again.

''I know.'' She reached out to stroke him.

''And you enjoyed every minute of it,'' he said as he claimed her, with hands and lips and tongue.

She arched her back as he made his way to the sweet ripeness of her breasts. ''Oh, yes.''

''And now,'' he said, taking the tantalizingly aroused peak into his mouth, ''it's my turn to be bad.''

Lily hadn't imagined Fletcher would be ready to make love to her again quite that soon. She gripped his shoulders, hard, trembling at the way he was pleasuring her. "Want me to put my outfit back on?"

"Later," he promised, pausing only long enough to shrug out of his shirt and toss it onto the floor with the rest of his discarded clothing. He ran his palms over her shoulders and down her forearms. "Right now I want to learn every inch of your body all over again. Do unto others, you know...."

She laughed softly as he tickled her ribs, brushed his lips across hers and took her earlobe between his teeth. "I never imagined making love could be so much fun."

He kissed his way back down her body, suffusing her with heat. He grazed her nipples with his thumbs, then slid his thigh along hers, easing them apart. "I had no idea, either."

He stroked along the inside of her thighs. "I mean, I knew it would be passionate," Lily rasped as he continued his sensual exploration of her body. She shuddered as he slipped two fingers inside her. "And I hoped it would be exciting, but—"

He rubbed and stroked in a way that was too outrageous and erotic for words until her insides clenched, asking for more, and sweet, hot liquid flowed. "No slam-bam-thank-you-ma'ams in your future?"

She took another breath and opened her eyes to look into his. She knew he was taunting her, the way she had taunted him, and she was enjoying every second of it. Not that she planned to let him know that. Yet. "I should say not," she informed with exaggerated hauteur, daring him to try and arouse her any more. "I want a man who knows how to take his time."

He grinned, as if he knew just the way. "I guess I should work on that." He slid both hands beneath her and lightly squeezed her buttocks in his palms. "You know what they say."

Lily gasped again as he touched her. "What?"

"Practice makes perfect." Gathering her close, he rolled so she was on top of him and kissed her again, deeply, passionately.

"That's—pretty darn close." She felt his manhood pulsing against her, poised to enter.

"Mmmm. I don't know, Lily." Parting her knees with his, he settled more deeply between her, his hands on her hips, lifting and positioning her. "I think I could do better."

As his mouth found her again, she practically shot off the bed. And this time it was she who was holding on to the headboard, shuddering, as her emotions skyrocketed and the climax she'd felt minutes before came roaring back. She moaned and bucked and he brought her back down to just below his waist.

"Now see?" he said playfully, as he stroked her again with his hand. "That's the kind of response I was looking for."

Lily trembled all the harder, all playfulness forgotten, her desire for him as intense as the feelings swelling in her heart. "Fletcher?"

"Hmmm?"

She cupped his shoulders and settled more intimately over him, beginning to wonder how she had ever managed without him. "I want you inside me."

He looked at her tenderly. ''I want to be inside you, too.'' He reached for the condoms on the bed-side table and quickly sheathed himself.

The next thing she knew they were changing places once again and he was moving over her. His skin was hot as fire, his body quivering with the effort of his restraint, as he possessed her all over again with a passion and determination that took her breath away and sent her soaring once again into sweet hot pleasure.

As they lay together, trying to recover for the second time that night, Lily buried her head in the warmth and strength of Fletcher's chest. He felt so good against her, so right. She realized she had never been happier in her life, and Fletcher seemed to feel that way, too.

Not wanting the moment to get too serious, however, lest she scare him away and ruin the best time she'd ever had with the best man she had ever known, Lily filled the silence with a joke she had been waiting her whole life to make.

''Well, I think I've found her.'' Lily sighed contentedly against Fletcher's shoulder as she stroked imaginary patterns on his chest.

Fletcher lifted his head, his eyes still dark with wanting her. ''Who?''

''My inner bad girl.''

Fletcher rolled, so Lily was on her back. His eyes were gentler than she had ever seen them, his look more protective. ''I'm glad,'' he told her warmly. ''I want all your wishes to come true.''

There was just one more....

And it was an important one.

I love you, Fletcher, Lily thought. And I *think* you love me. But unsure how such a wildly passionate and deeply honest revelation like that would be received, unsure of what his intentions truly were, she once again kept silent and merely cuddled closer, enjoying the feel of his warm strong arms wrapped around her.

Chapter Eleven

"You're sure you want to do this?" Fletcher asked at 5:45 a.m. as Lily was getting ready to go to work.

Lily had wondered when the subject of Carson McRue Productions would come up. She didn't want anything to come between them after the wonderful night they'd had. But she also knew this was a precedent-setting situation with Fletcher and she was prepared to stand her ground. Even under fire.

"It's a 'piece of cake' job, Fletcher," she told him softly. "They've already ordered the greenery and calla lilies through a Hollywood florist they've got on retainer. They had them delivered to my shop late yesterday afternoon. The set designer came up with the placement and style of arrangements for the chapel. All I have to do is show up there in fifteen minutes and put things together as per direction, in time for them to get started with the filming around eight. It's not very hard."

Fletcher shot her a quelling glance. "Then why do it?" he asked mildly.

Lily had promised herself when her grandmother

Rose passed that her days of answering to someone about every little thing she did were over. But something in Fletcher's eyes—concern or something deeper—had her wanting to put his mind at ease. Especially since she knew he was trying to protect her, not fence her in.

Lily tried hard not to notice how handsome Fletcher looked, lounging in the mussed covers of her bed, a coffee cup propped on his knee. "Because they've offered me a five-thousand-dollar fee for a couple of hours of work. All I had to do was agree to do it all myself."

Fletcher's jaw set. "So in other words you're going to be at the church alone," he deduced.

Lily did not like the hint of reproof in his low voice. "No." She turned to the mirror as she ran a brush through the still-damp layers of her curly blond hair, wondering if she looked as well loved to the uniformed observer as she felt. "There will be other people there," she stated firmly.

Fletcher's brow lifted. "Sure?"

Lily paused, lipstick in hand as the first inkling of doubt crept in. Carson McRue would not be doing all of this simply to get a chance to make a pass at her. Would he?

"It's not just the flowers that have to be done this morning," Lily persisted, even though she risked Fletcher's ire. "They have to set up the cameras, too." She spritzed on some perfume and bent to put on her shoes.

Fletcher stood and moved away from the bed

where they'd made love over and over through the night. He was clad in jeans, but his shirt lay open, baring his beautifully muscled chest, bronzed skin and mat of golden-brown hair. "Let me go with you."

Lily flushed beneath his quick but potent scrutiny. If he only knew how tempted she was to let him do just that....

"I don't need a bodyguard." *I'm a grown woman, capable of managing on my own.* "Besides, you were fired yesterday and escorted from the set, remember?" The last thing either of them needed was a scene. Lily might be trying to ditch her Ice Princess rep, but she did not want to be the focus of gossip. She had already experienced that the past couple of weeks. It hadn't been pleasant and she had no desire to repeat it.

"If no one else is going to be there, except the camera people, who's to know?" Fletcher asked.

Carson McRue, Lily thought. The arrogant actor would punish Fletcher. If for no other reason than Fletcher had publicly questioned Carson's ability to control that stallion yesterday....

Although tempted to accept his offer for reasons she couldn't quite understand, Lily shook her head. "You could do one thing for me, though," she said as she sashayed toward him and clasped the open edges of his shirt.

"Make love to you again?"

Lily went weak in the knees at just the thought. "If we were to start that again," she murmured, lay-ing her head against his shoulder, "I'd never get to work."

"Yeah. But think of all the fun we'd have." Fletcher wrapped his arms around her and brought her fully against him. Tucking a hand beneath her chin, he delivered a long leisurely kiss as Spartacus padded into the bedroom to join them.

"I'm serious," Lily persisted as a sensual shiver slid down her spine. "I need someone to feed and walk Spartacus for me this morning."

"I'll do it," he murmured against her mouth, kissing her again.

"You sure?" Lily asked as his gaze ardently traced her face, lingering on each feature in turn.

Drawing back, Fletcher nodded. "Spartacus can come to work with me." A smile broke across his face as talk turned to their canine friend. Still holding her gaze, he inclined his head slightly to the side, shot a fond look at Spartacus then returned his attention to Lily. "It's about time I had a dog in my life again. Wouldn't you say?"

TWO GRUELING HOURS later, Lily had Unity Church exactly the way the *Hollywood P.I.* set designer wanted it to look. Finished, she began packing up her gear in the toolbox she took with her on location jobs. She returned the leftover greenery, satin ribbon and calla lilies to the set designer's assistant, who immediately corrected her mistake.

"You're supposed to take those to Carson McRue's trailer."

Lily blinked. "Excuse me?"

The set designer shrugged. "He wanted a couple arrangements to brighten up the place."

A trickle of unease ran through Lily at the suspect nature of the request. "I didn't bring any vases."

"That's okay." The set designer looked distracted as she pushed a hand through her hair. "He's probably got a few extra in there. If not, he'll either send you out for some or make do." The set designer rushed off to help with the rolling out of the bridal carpet.

She could handle this, even if Carson made a pass. Hadn't she told Fletcher that? Well, now was the time to prove herself, Lily thought, as she dodged lighting and camera guys who were also setting up, and headed out to Carson's trailer. Holding the armload of flowers to her chest, she moved across the square and saw the crowd, who knew from reports on the local news that the wedding scenes from the show's November sweeps episodes were going to be filmed that morning.

It had stopped raining during the night, but the ground was saturated and the creek that ran through the city park across the street was swollen with rushing brown water. Out of the corner of her eye, she saw Fletcher standing next to his brother Mac. Fletcher had Spartacus on a leash and was looking her way. Mac was busy with his sheriff's duties, keeping onlookers back from the barricades. In the center of the square, was the horse trailer, the rowdy stallion and what Lily could only presume was the veterinary consultant hired to replace Fletcher.

She noticed Fletcher's frown as she hurried over to Carson's trailer. He didn't like this. Well, neither did she. And as soon as she dumped these flowers, she was out of there. Maybe in time to get some breakfast with Fletcher. As she neared the steps leading up to the trailer, the security person standing just outside looked at her with something akin to contempt. "Carson is waiting for you."

Taking a deep breath, Lily squared her shoulders and went on in.

Carson was seated on the rich leather sofa. He was dressed in a tuxedo shirt and tie and looked as handsome as any screen idol she had ever seen. "I was told you wanted floral arrangements in here?" Lily adapted her crispest, most professional tone.

Carson nodded. He gestured to several vases, filled with perfectly good flowers placed about the living room and kitchen area of the trailer. "You can use those. There's one in the bedroom, too."

"All right." Refusing to meet his eyes or make this situation any more intimate than it already was, Lily gathered them up, reminding herself all the while that there was a five-thousand-dollar fee attached to her work this morning that would go a long way toward making the redecoration of her home possible. "Is it all right if I work in the kitchen area," she asked impersonally, "or would you like me to take them out and bring them back when they're done?"

"Here's fine." Carson didn't lift his eyes from the script in front of him.

Maybe her imagination was running away from her. Maybe all he wanted from her were fresh flowers in vases.

Aware that the hair on the back of her neck was standing up, she was so on edge, Lily nevertheless got down to business and went to work. In ten minutes, she had all the flowers replaced, the old ones in a garbage bag she was prepared to take with her. "You're all set," she told Carson as she headed for the door.

He looked up from the page he was studying, then nodded his thanks. "Listen," he said, as she reached the door, "could you do me a favor?"

Uh-oh. Lily turned toward him, suddenly wishing Fletcher were here, with her. "How can I help you?" she asked in the most impersonal voice she could manage.

"Run some lines with me. I'm having a heck of a time with this dialogue this morning."

She waved off the request. "I'm no actress."

Carson moved toward her in a way that suggested he was not going to take no for an answer. "All you have to do is say Sylvia's lines." He took the garbage bag of discarded blossoms from her, put it aside and thrust the script in her hands. "Right here." He gave her a brief, detached smile as he pointed where he wanted her to start.

Lily looked down at the script. It was the scene in

the chapel where the two married. "Shouldn't your costar be doing this?" she asked.

Carson shook his head. "She's not speaking to me. Hasn't been since yesterday. Actresses." He rolled his eyes.

"Right." Lily looked down at the page, lamenting all the while that Fletcher had been right. And wouldn't he just crow about that…? *Just get it over with. And get out of here.* She cleared her throat and read in a rote, choppy tone, "'Honestly, Rex, I do love you.'"

"'But?'" Carson stepped nearer, slid a hand beneath her chin. Lifting her face to his, he searched her eyes. Flustered, Lily stepped back, ducked her head and continued reading from the script in the most staccato robotic voice she could manage. "'I just don't know that this is the right thing for either of us.'"

Suddenly Carson's hands were cupping her shoulders. Startled to find him touching her again, she dropped her script and looked up at him.

"'But it is, Sylvia,'" Carson murmured, and then his head was lowering.

Lily had a millionth of a second and then he was going to kiss her.

So Lily did the only thing she could. She raised her sneaker-clad foot and stepped as hard as she could on the arrogant actor's instep.

"I'M TELLING YOU," Fletcher said to his brother Mac as he continued staring grimly at Carson McRue's trailer. "One more minute and I'm going in after her."

"Something tells me Lily Madsen would *not* appreciate that," Mac murmured, once again motioning spectators with cameras and camcorders back from the barricades.

Mac turned and gave Fletcher a hard look.

Guilt flooded Fletcher.

"Oh, man." Mac sighed, shaking his head as he correctly deduced what was really going on between Lily and Fletcher.

Fletcher lifted a palm. "Don't judge," he warned.

Mac did, anyway. Perhaps because his law-and-order personality would not allow him to do otherwise. "You're doing the stupidest thing you could possibly do, aren't you?" Mac grumbled, sounding like the head of the family he had become after their father's death twenty years before. Mac narrowed his eyes in obvious disapproval. "You're getting involved with her."

Getting? Fletcher thought. He and Lily were way past that. She was part of his life now.

"At least tell me you haven't taken her to bed," Mac continued sternly.

Fletcher never had been able to lie to Mac.

Conscience prickling, not for making love to her but for ever having involved her in a bet with his brothers, however unknowingly, Fletcher turned his attention to the horse being saddled up. Overhead, storm clouds were threatening once again. "That stallion is dangerous," Fletcher said, changing the subject adroitly. "You really need to get everyone out of here."

Mac looked at the nervous, prancing horse and took Fletcher at his word. "You really think someone will get hurt?" Mac asked.

Fletcher nodded grimly, just as the door to Carson McRue's trailer opened. "What in blazes...?" Fletcher murmured as Lily came storming out.

She looked exactly as she had when she had gone in, except her cheeks were bright red and she looked angrier and more upset than Fletcher had ever seen her. "That son of a bitch," Fletcher swore again as Lily crossed the square. Behind her, Carson McRue strode out, too, looking as debonair in a tuxedo as James Bond.

The director motioned to Carson and then the stallion. "We want to get these horse shots filmed now before it starts raining again!" the director said through his megaphone.

For once, Fletcher could have cared less about that. Taking Spartacus's leash, he moved to cut Lily off as she stepped around the barricades. "What happened?" he demanded.

Lily blushed all the harder and looked away. "Not here." She pushed the words through clenched teeth, refusing to look him in the eye. "Not now."

Fletcher caught her arm. "I swear, if McRue so much as looked at you funny, I'm going to go punch him out," he whispered furiously in her ear.

"Oh, please! I've had enough of stupid men for

one day!'' Lily grabbed Spartacus's leash and wove her way through the crowd.

Fletcher stared after her, unsure whether to pursue her or just go and have it out with the arrogant actor right then and there. ''Lily's right. Don't make a scene,'' Mac advised as the director called, ''Action!'' Carson took a running start toward the prancing stallion and jumped into the saddle with a stuntman's ease. Another actor rushed from the chapel, a fake pistol in his hand. Everyone gasped as the second tuxedo-clad actor fired repeatedly at Carson and the horse. And then, just as Fletcher had predicted, all hell broke loose as the stallion—unaccustomed to TV stunt work—went wild.

LILY WAS STILL cursing herself for her naiveté and winding her way through the hike and bike trails that ran parallel to the creek when she heard what sounded like gunshots. Startled, she and Spartacus both turned in the direction of the sound, and the screams of genuine terror that followed. She was shocked to find a thundering horse and ineptly out-of-control rider headed her way. For a second, Lily stood there transfixed by sheer terror, unable to move. And then she came to her senses and she and Spartacus both leapt out of the way.

Carson and the stallion that Fletcher had fought against using thundered past, knocking both Lily and her dog off balance. Lily had another second of mind-numbing panic, and then she and her dog were both slip-sliding on the mossy slope that lined the creek bank, losing their footing.

Lily knew she was going to fall—and probably drown, as well—in the rushing, churning brown water. She was damned if she was taking poor Spartacus in with her. So she did the only thing she could do. She let go of the leash. Made one last desperate attempt to save herself. And failed miserably.

Fletcher was already running toward her when Lily tumbled head over heels into the rushing creek. Dammit. Dammit! "Get a rope!" he yelled at Mac, his heart failing as he saw Lily bob up once, go back under, come up again and then go under and stay under.

Spartacus leaned over the bank, a lot more sure-footed than the sneaker-clad Lily had been. He was barking at the water where she had disappeared as Fletcher ran faster than he thought possible to rapidly close the distance between them. Still the seconds were ticking by and no Lily. Suddenly Spartacus was diving in after her and going underwater. Fletcher took off his shoes and dove in, too. Moments later, Spartacus bobbed up, the T-shirt of the unconscious Lily clamped firmly in his jaws.

Fletcher fought the current that was already sweeping them all downstream as Spartacus struggled to paddle toward him.

Please, God, he prayed, desperately. Please…don't take her from me, too.

Spartacus and Lily went under once again. Fletcher swam harder, determined to save them. And then a miracle happened. Spartacus bobbed up, Lily's shirt still clamped in his powerful jaws. Fletcher let out a shout of relief and gave a mighty push through the wall of water separating them. And then the three of them were locked together, he and Spartacus working together to keep from being swept under the swirling current as they struggled to hold the still-unconscious, gray-skinned Lily's head above water.

They got pushed downstream anyway, Fletcher's back scraping against exposed tree roots. Spartacus took a pounding, too. And then Mac was there above them, lasso in hand, yelling at them to hang on. Throwing them a rope.

His heart pounding, Fletcher held Lily all the tighter, praying it wasn't too late.

Chapter Twelve

Lily came to with the stormy gray sky above her, the hard ground beneath her and a rough canine tongue frantically licking her hand. As she struggled to focus, she saw Fletcher's face above her. He looked as if he had taken a dunking—his clothes were wet, his hair and face dripping with muddy water—and that quickly she recalled falling into the creek herself. Panicking all over again, she reached out.

"It's okay, Lily," he reassured her, his voice gruff with emotion. As she looked into his eyes, she saw they were filled with tears. And so, she realized belatedly, were hers.

"I'm here. And so is Spartacus. We've got you." Fletcher gripped her hand as two guys in EMS uniforms worked over her.

Realizing that she was indeed safe, Lily caught a glimpse of Spartacus lying to the left of her. Also drenched, he had his handsome white-blond head on his paws, watching her, and indeed looked okay. Relief flowed through her, as well as the immediate need to comfort her pet as Fletcher was comforting her. She coughed, choking on the worst water she had ever tasted in her life, and struggled to sit up to get to him. "Just take it easy," one of the EMS workers told her, forcibly easing her back. "You had quite a tumble there."

Lily felt it in every inch of her body. And more importantly, she felt alive. *Fletcher,* she thought, locking eyes with him. *I love you.* And she could have sworn by the way he looked at her that he loved her, too.

"Dr. Hart and that dog saved your life," one of the EMS workers continued cheerfully as they listened to her lungs and checked her pulse.

Lily smiled weakly, watching as Fletcher reached over and petted Spartacus with his other hand, the gratitude and love she felt easing her ravaged senses. "No surprise there," Lily murmured with a weak smile, gripping Fletcher's palm even tighter. Those two guys were her heart. And then some.

A few hours later, Lily was being released from the Holly Springs Medical Center. Fletcher was there to take her home, and the still-shaken Lily had never been so glad in her life to see anyone waiting for her.

"You heard the doc," Fletcher said, still looking as wet and uncomfortable as Lily felt in her damp and dirty clothing. He held her against him and squeezed her as if he never wanted to let her go. "You need rest."

"And a shower." Lily sighed, knowing she must look a fright.

He clamped his arm tighter around her waist, looking as eager to give her tender loving care as she was grateful to receive it. And that was a surprise. Lily had never dreamed she would ever need—or want—a man this much. And Fletcher, bless his courageous soul, seemed to be struggling with the same wealth of feelings. Gratitude, that they'd survived. Anger, that any of them had ever been endangered in the first place. As well as the need to connect again, to reassure themselves that whatever this was that they had was not going to be taken away. Not now, not ever.

"My place okay?" Fletcher asked, the emotion in his low, husky voice counter to the studied casualness of his words. He leaned over and kissed her temple. "It's closer to the hospital."

"Sounds perfect," Lily murmured as Spartacus stuck his head out of the open window of Fletcher's pickup truck and let out a welcoming bark.

Fletcher helped Lily into the passenger seat, while Spartacus hopped in the cargo space behind the front seat. Spartacus smelled like creek water, too. And thank heaven he did, Lily thought, since it had taken both of them to keep her alive.

Fletcher still looked worried as he drove the short distance to his apartment above the animal clinic. Lily did what she could to lighten the mood and put aside the close call they had all shared. "Well, you finally got to see me in a wet T-shirt," Lily teased.

Fletcher shot her a look as she plucked the damp fabric away from her breasts. "Not the way I would have ordered it up," he said just as dryly.

"I know." *God help me, I know...*

He parked and helped her out of the truck and up

the steps into his place. Lily leaned against him, appreciating his warmth and his strength. Once he had her safely inside, he sat her down at the table. Spartacus, satisfied all was well, collapsed in a heap on the kitchen floor and put his head on his paws. Fletcher walked over to get him a dog biscuit and knelt down to rub the Labrador retriever's head. "You're a hero. And you deserve more than this." He put the biscuit in front of him. "So it's steak tonight for all of us. Okay, buddy?"

Spartacus's liquid-brown eyes radiated understanding and love.

Fletcher grinned, rubbed the dog's head affectionately once again, then stood and came over to stand in front of Lily. "You want to get a shower? Or rest first?"

Lily's knees were still a little wobbly—whether from the accident or anticipation of the lovemaking to come—she didn't know. But she couldn't imagine climbing into the sheets with creek grit still clinging to her skin and hair. "Shower," Lily said.

Fletcher looked as if he had expected her to say just that. His arm around her waist, they walked into the bedroom. "You know," she quipped, trying not to think how right this felt or how easily she could get used to being cared for like this. "I think there have been days where we've both smelled better."

Fletcher feigned bafflement and stuck his nose in his armpit. "I don't know," he declared with a solemn face. "I might have smelled worse a time or two."

Lily supposed that was true, him being a guy and all. "Well, I haven't," she said primly.

She lifted her arms and let him help her take her long-sleeved T-shirt off. He narrowed his eyes at the angry red scrapes and purpling bruises on her shoulders, arms and rib cage.

"I'm okay, Fletcher," Lily reminded him. "Just a little banged-up from getting knocked around by the rushing water."

"No thanks to that jerk of an actor who mowed you down and knocked you into the creek." Fletcher looked as though he wanted to punch Carson McRue's lights out.

"Can we forget about him?" Lily pushed her hands through her hair. She had.

"Not until you answer me one question," Fletcher said, the calmness in his voice at odds with his hawklike gaze. He moved in even closer. His voice might have been calm, but his eyes were hot. "What exactly happened between the two of you in that trailer?"

For a second, Fletcher thought Lily wasn't going to answer him. Then her expression changed and her guard lowered. "He started to make a really cheesy pass at me," she explained as if it were no big deal and happened to her all the time—and maybe, Fletcher thought, it did. "So I stomped on his instep as hard as I possibly could. He yelped. I told him what I thought of his manners—not much. Called him a few unprintable names. And took off."

Fletcher couldn't help but admire her decisive kick-butt reaction to the unwanted attention, even as unaccustomed jealousy roiled inside him. Lily was his woman, damn it. The sooner everyone realized that, the better. "That's why you left his trailer in such a hurry," Fletcher supposed.

"Yep." Lily toed off her sneakers and water-logged socks. "If I'd stayed one second longer, I would have knocked him flat."

Fletcher watched as she shimmied out of her damp jeans. She was wearing panties with flowers on them. "I'd still be happy to do it for you," he offered.

To Fletcher's disappointment, Lily did not look as if she found it necessary for him to further defend her honor. Her glance turned pitying as they continued to talk about the man who had nearly cost Lily her life. "I think he's suffered enough, don't you?"

Fletcher looked at Lily blankly. He had no clue what she meant.

Realizing this, Lily explained, "One of the spectators caught it all on videotape. Him losing control of the horse, looking like an idiot. While I was at the hospital, a reporter called, wanting to know my condition. The E.R. doc asked if he could tell the TV station I was being treated and released. I said okay to that but no to an interview with Trevor Zwick at W-MOL Action News. I imagine right about now Carson McRue is busy doing damage control and '*rue*ing' the day he ever tried to make time with me. Because this has got to hurt his suave hero image."

"Very true." Fletcher couldn't help but be pleased about that. The footage would probably be replayed endlessly on tabloid television shows. Repeated assaults on Carson McRue's pride would indeed be some punishment for what he had done. But not nearly enough, Fletcher thought, as he remembered all over again how scared he had been when he had watched Lily falling into the rain-swollen creek and going under...

"Fletcher," Lily warned as she stepped out of her panties and unfastened her bra. "You do not need to hit him on my behalf."

Trying to be gallant rather than lecherous—a pretty hard proposition given how damn beautiful Lily looked right now, standing there in the altogether—Fletcher leaned past her to turn on the shower and adjust it to just the right temperature for her. "I'll be the judge of that," Fletcher said, deciding a sock in the jaw was exactly what that pretty boy needed to make him think twice before ever needlessly endangering anyone again.

"Fletcher!" Lily warned, reading his mind as easily as ever.

"Fine," Fletcher relented, amazed to find himself taking the high road. "As long as Carson McRue never comes near either of us again, I will not punch his lights out." Although he sure would have enjoyed doing so.

"Thank you." Lily released a sigh of relief and stepped into the glass-and-tile-walled shower stall. Bruised and pale she was still the loveliest thing Fletcher had ever seen. He handed her a washcloth and looped a towel over the top of the shower door, within easy reach. "Anything else you need?" he asked, reluctantly preparing to make himself scarce.

"Yes," Lily said, hooking her hand in the front

of his shirt and dragging him near. For the first time
in two hours, the smile on her lips matched the one
in her eyes. "You."

Lily had had a lot of experience being the Ice Princess of Holly Springs but not much chance to be a
femme fatale. It was amazingly easy to get the hang
of it, she discovered, when Fletcher Hart was her
targeted male.

"Lily," Fletcher warned as she tugged him inside
the stall with her.

"Yeah, yeah, I know." She watched the surprise
come into his eyes, the desire. And knew even
though he was bound to resist her out of some misguided sense of chivalry, that the battle was already
won. Grinning saucily, she began undoing the buttons on his shirt. She let the backs of her hands brush
the warmth of his chest and felt his muscles tense.
"If you come in here and get naked with me you're
going to want to make love to me."

"Exactly." Fletcher's eyes darkened to molten
gold as she tugged the hem from the waistband of
his jeans. Opening up the fabric of his shirt, she
stepped inside it, bringing her body flush with his
and letting her breasts brush against his skin. As her
nipples tightened into tight buds of arousal, she
moaned, a soft helpless little sound in the back of
her throat. She smiled with satisfaction when she felt
his lower body harden.

"Well, that's what I want," Lily said, already
looping a hand around his neck and guiding his face
down to hers. "You know what they say about neardeath experiences." She pressed her lips to his,

clinging to him and kissing him the way she had wanted to kiss him from the moment she had awakened and found herself lying on the ground beside him. She'd known in that instant that if not for his courage—and the courage of the dog she'd finally decided to adopt—she would not have made it. "All they really make you want to do is live," she murmured as one of his hands opened over her back, guiding her closer, and the other cupped her chin.

And live they did. As he passionately returned her kiss, desire wreaked havoc through their entire systems. But even that contact wasn't enough. Impatient to have him as naked—and thereby accessible to her questing hands, as she was to his—she stepped back, helped him off with his shirt…and saw his resistance flare.

He kissed her hard, but much too briefly, on the mouth. "You know this is going to confirm a damning lack of chivalry on my part, don't you?" His voice was husky, his amber eyes bright. "Especially since the doctor said what you really needed to do was just rest."

"And I will," Lily persisted, helping him off with his jeans, making sure he knew by her look she really wanted this to happen. "Later."

"Lily." Fletcher groaned again as her hands slid inside his boxer-briefs and pushed those down, too. He continued to resist passively even as he kissed her neck, her throat, the top of her head.

"Fletcher." She playfully mocked his tone, his disapproving look.

When she had him naked, too, she straightened.

She could see he was still having qualms about what she wanted them to do. He was still set on doing the right thing, especially where she was concerned. The old Lily would have just let the guy call the shots—even if they were the wrong ones. However, the new and improved Lily knew it was okay to have needs and wants of her own—and to act on those desires, no matter how inappropriate they might seem to someone else. Fletcher wasn't resisting her; he was trying to help her and would in fact do anything to help her feel better. She just had to let Fletcher know what the right thing in this situation was. Acutely aware of the myriad feelings running riot inside her, she gathered all her courage and took his hand, laid it across her breasts. "Feel my heart," she whispered urgently, still aching for him to touch her.

Fletcher's eyes darkened with a mixture of affection and awe. "It's racing."

"But not just any old way," she announced flirtatiously. She moved her lower torso in even closer until it rested against his, and she could feel the depth of his arousal. "With excitement."

Fletcher grinned, his knowledge of basic biology coming into play. "With unused adrenaline."

"Exactly." Lily nodded. She kissed him again, the kiss feeling like a commitment, a bridge to their future. "And can you think of any better way to work it off?" she finished triumphantly, looking deep into his eyes. "Especially after we all had such a close call?"

Fletcher didn't know what he had done to deserve a woman like Lily. He didn't care. All he knew was that somehow over the course of protecting her, he had fallen head over heels in love with her. To the point that he could no longer imagine his life without her. And as soon as things calmed down, he was going to have to do something about that. Something definitive, like propose. But for now all he really wanted to do, now that she had worked so hard to convince him she really was up to it, was make love to her as gently and thoroughly as possible. And the first thing they had to do in that regard was get the creek grit off of both of them.

"I don't know how good I'm going to be at this...." he murmured as he grabbed the bottle of baby shampoo and poured some into his palm. He had never washed a woman's hair before. Never told a woman he loved her. And the cynical side of him had to wonder how she would take the news. Would she immediately tell him that she loved him, too? As he hoped. Or get a panicked look and tell him she needed time. To be on her own. To live without comment or protection...

Not that it mattered, Fletcher reassured himself as he deftly worked the lather through Lily's damp curls. He knew he could be patient when he needed to be. The only thing that really mattered was what happened in the end, and about that he had no doubt. He and Lily were going to get married. And have a houseful of kids and pets and dual careers and make each other's dreams come true.

"Since the only person's hair I'm used to shampooing is mine," Fletcher continued out loud, already thinking about all the ways he was going to drive her wild. Because although Lily might look like innocence defined, at heart she was all passionate woman. And she needed him as much as he needed her, even if she hadn't quite come out and admitted it yet.

Lily grinned and closed her eyes as she sank into his touch. "Good thing it's tear-free, then," she quipped.

Fletcher chuckled, enjoying the anticipation of making love to her almost as much as he was going to savor claiming her as his. "You'll have your turn." He reached for the handheld showerhead and gently began rinsing the lather from her scalp, enjoying the way she surrendered herself to him. "'Cause I'm going to let you do mine."

Looking as if she could stay there with him forever, Lily pressed her lips to his damp skin, then rested her cheek on his forearm. "Then it'll be a first for me, too," she said as he soaped her body from head to toe, lingering on her breasts, buttocks and thighs before zeroing in on the most intimate place of all.

"Keep this up," she told him breathlessly as she reached for the shampoo and poured some in her palm, "and we'll never make it to the bed."

"Okay with me," Fletcher said, inclining his head to the left so she could more easily reach and shampoo his hair. He winked as she swayed toward him, wanting more. "I like you wet."

"Same here, bucko. Same here." Taking her time, she soaped him down and rinsed him with the showerhead. She worked efficiently at first. Then, a lot less efficiently, until they had a playful battle over the spray that ended with both of them getting doused liberally in the face and breaking into laughter. And then just as abruptly, playtime was over. His lips were locked on hers, her mouth pliant beneath his, her body soft and surrendering. Loving the way she responded to him—yielding sweetly to him one moment, ardently taking control the next—Fletcher put everything he had into the steamy caress, stroking and touching her, making her his. Until she was trembling, falling apart in his hands, moaning softly, urging him to love her then and there. Unable to deny her anything, he kissed her long and hard and deep, leaving no question about the depth of his need for her.

Love filled her eyes as he eased her back against the tile wall and settled between her legs. Their lips met and he kissed her again, until there was no doubt how much they needed each other. His manhood pressed against her inner thighs as he molded her breasts with his hands, teasing her nipples into pearling buds. Lily strained against him, undulating impatiently. Determined to give her everything he needed, he held on, making his way south, kissing her breathless and exploring damp silky flesh until she was clutching him closer and climaxing all over again.

Lily could feel the wildness in Fletcher matching the untamed part of her, and desperate to have him inside her once again—filling her completely—she went up on tiptoe in an effort to better accommodate him. He moaned, needing her, too, and sliding his hands beneath her hips, lifted her higher still. She gasped at the feel of him poised so hot and hard against her. And then, with one bold but gentle thrust, they were blissfully connected. The tile wall was against her back and he was as deep inside of her as he could be. Stroking and tantalizing, giving, taking. Demanding. Accepting. Engulfing her with tenderness and giving her his all.

Her eyes closed, Lily let her head fall back. She loved the feel of him. The scent of him. The way he was inside her, slowly, inexorably, claiming her as his, giving her untold pleasure even as he painstakingly sought out his own. She loved the womanly way he made her feel, the freedom he gave her just to be. She loved him. Just the way he was. And it was a secret that was nearly too much to bear....

Afterward, he dried her off and took her to bed. She knew he wanted her to go straight to sleep, but there were things she needed to say. Too much had happened to simply let it go without comment, she thought, as she cuddled close to him, resting her head on his chest and listening to the strong steady beat of his heart. "You were my hero today, you know. You and Spartacus, both." She shut her eyes, trying not to think about how near all three of them had come to death. Emotion tightened her throat as she pushed away the anxiety that lingered. "I wouldn't have survived without you."

Fletcher stroked his hands through the dampness of her just-washed hair, his touch as compelling and sure as his lovemaking had been. "No surprise there," he murmured huskily, kissing the top of her head, stroking her back. Tenderness filled his eyes. "No way were we going to let anything happen to you."

"Well, you didn't." Lily snuggled closer, inhaling the clean, soapy fragrance of his skin. *Don't rock the boat. Don't say anything that Fletcher might regret.* "And for that I'll be forever grateful."

Looking as happy to be there with her as she was to be with him, Fletcher rolled, so she was beneath him. He kissed her and they made love again, sweetly and slowly this time, before finally drifting off to sleep wrapped in each other's arms.

When Lily awakened, the alarm was going off. She blinked, disoriented, as Fletcher reached over and shut it off. The clock said six-thirty, and the room was filled with dusky light. Outside, they could hear the rain pouring down once again. Lily rolled onto her side, still trying to figure out what day it was. "Did we sleep all night?" she asked drowsily, rubbing her eyes.

Fletcher shook his head. He looked as if he could spend a lot longer in bed, too, but forced himself to sit up anyway. "Just all afternoon. I set the alarm because we have Janey and Thad's wedding rehearsal and dinner this evening." He searched her face. "Do you feel up to going? I'm sure they would understand if you didn't, under the circumstances."

"No. I want to go." Lily sat up, moving stiffly, stretched. She studied him, too. "Don't you?"

Fletcher nodded. To her relief, he looked as happy to be participating in his sister Janey's wedding, as

Lily felt. "But I've got to go home," Lily continued. "Get my clothes and do my hair and all that."

"Give me ten minutes to shave and get ready myself and then I'll drive you," Fletcher promised.

"DON'T YOU TWO LOOK lovey-dovey," Hannah Reid noted as Lily and Fletcher entered the church where the wedding rehearsal was going to take place.

"Yeah," Joe's wife, Emma, demanded with a wink and a smile as she came up to stand beside them. "Who's getting married here tomorrow anyway?"

"Thad and me?" Janey continued the teasing playfully as she handed out "bouquets" for the bridesmaids to practice with. "Or Sir Galahad and the damsel in distress he rescued?"

Lily turned to Fletcher proudly and was shocked to see that for the first time that day Fletcher looked uncomfortable with the role he had played in pulling her out of the rising waters of Holly Creek.

He held up both hands in a gesture of surrender. "Don't go making me out to be a hero," he said gruffly, something akin to guilt flashing across his face before promptly disappearing once again.

"But you were one," Lily protested, frustrated that Fletcher still did not see himself as she saw him. As the bravest, most decent man in the whole world. "Because if you hadn't jumped in when you did—" she continued earnestly.

Once again, Fletcher couldn't quite look her in the eye as he cut her off with an abrupt shake of his head. "Someone else would have saved you," he told her curtly.

As the rest of Fletcher's brothers gathered around, Lily noticed all four of the Hart brothers—save Dylan, who wasn't there—and Janey's fiancé, Thad, were suddenly looking at Fletcher a little oddly. As if they all knew something she didn't. And perhaps should.

"Is there something going on I ought to know about?" Lily asked slowly.

More telltale scuffling of shoes. Looking everywhere but at her.

"No," every man in the room said abruptly and in unison. To Lily's dismay, Janey and Emma looked uncomfortable, too. Only Susan Hart and Hannah Reid looked as in the dark as Lily as to what could possibly be going on. And that was, Lily found, small comfort. Again, Lily felt a little niggling of doubt. Deliberately, she pushed it away. Nothing was going to ruin her blossoming relationship with Fletcher, or the feelings she had for him....

Fortunately, the minister arrived, and the rehearsal started soon after. To everyone's delight, it went off without a hitch, as did the catered rehearsal dinner back at Thad's home and the traditional giving out of gifts to members of the wedding party, by Janey and Thad. Fletcher was polite, funny, attentive to her every need. But whenever he thought she wasn't looking, he regarded her with something Lily could only identify as guilt or regret of some sort.

Was he sorry he had made love to her? Lily wondered. Sorry he had become so involved? Tired of her already and getting ready to dump her? Much to her frustration, she had no clue what was going on with him and could only pretend she was as cool and composed as Fletcher appeared to be.

Finally, it was time to leave. Fletcher drove Lily back to her place and walked her to the door. They could see Spartacus—who had been left with a pet-sitter that evening—waiting by the window. The pet-sitter, who cared for many of Fletcher's canine patients in the owners' absence, came forward to give them an update about the events of the evening. "He never stopped waiting for the two of you to come back," she told Fletcher and Lily.

"But he was otherwise calm," Lily ascertained, noting that it didn't look as if Spartacus had been chewing on his paws again.

The pet-sitter nodded as Fletcher took his wallet out and paid her. "Spartacus didn't seem to need any reassurance from me at all," she said.

Lily thanked her and the pet-sitter left to drive home.

Fletcher bent down to pet and praise Spartacus for his good behavior, then turned back to Lily and observed proudly, "He obviously considers this his home now."

Lily nodded, pleased by Fletcher's observation, but still feeling a little wary. Was it her imagination or was Fletcher still on edge? And if so, why? What was it everyone had not wanted her to pick up on?

Fletcher stood. "Something on your mind?"

The old Lily would have let it go, rather than risk doing something so unladylike as to make a guest in her home uncomfortable. And though the cowardly part of Lily was tempted to do just that, rather than risk discovering a problem that would jeopardize her feelings for Fletcher, the new, assertive Lily knew she couldn't just pretend that everything was fine when it wasn't. Or behave as though it was going to be okay for Fletcher to keep secrets from her that clearly made him and everyone else around him uncomfortable. If their love was true—and Lily acknowledged on her part that it was—then it ought to be strong enough to handle whatever difficulty came their way.

She looked Fletcher straight in the eye. "What's the secret between you and your brothers?" she asked.

Chapter Thirteen

"You can't base a relationship on lies of omission," Joe had said. *"You have to tell Lily about the bet you made with us. Otherwise you risk her finding out some other way."*

Fletcher knew—as did his younger brother, Joe, who'd had his own problems caused by deliberately withheld information—that Lily would never forgive him if that happened. Fletcher could swear Thad and his brothers to secrecy, of course, but all it would take was one verbal slip or innocent but telling remark, by any of them, and then he would be in this exact same position again. So he had a choice. Either 'fess up and get it all out in the open and deal with the consequences now, whatever they might be. Or tell her it was nothing and have that lie and his guilt and fear of discovery continue to stand between them.

Lily was still regarding him expectantly. Aware it was time to own up to the reckless boast he wished like hell he had never made, Fletcher rubbed the tense muscles in the back of his neck. "You remember when you made a bet with your friends about Carson McRue?'' he said with obvious difficulty.

Lily nodded.

Emotion choking his throat, Fletcher told her, ''Well, I made a wager, too.''

As soon as the words were out, Lily went so still Fletcher could almost feel the chill that descended over her heart. ''What kind of wager?'' she asked warily.

Guilt flooded Fletcher anew, as he looked her straight in the eye and admitted with increasing uneasiness, ''The kind guys make to each other when they're at their most unruly. The kind I wished I could take back the moment the words were out of my mouth.'' But he hadn't, and now here they were.

Looking as if she suddenly needed to sit down, Lily moved to the living room and groped her way into a chair without ever taking her eyes from his.

Fletcher plunged on. ''I bet Thad and all four of my brothers—''

''Or in other words, all the male members of the wedding party,'' Lily interrupted.

Fletcher nodded. ''—that not only would you give up a date with Carson McRue but that you'd do it to go out with me.''

''I see.'' Lily continued staring at him as if he were a stranger. ''So all this attention—the rescuing, and making love to me—was to win a wager?'' she asked incredulously. ''That's why you refused to introduce me to Carson before he and the film crew hit town?''

Fletcher knew he could stop now. She already had

enough to resent him the rest of her natural-born days. But then he'd have to worry about her finding out about the rest.

"No," he said, swallowing hard around the ache in his throat as she balled her hands into fists. "My protecting you in that sense had nothing to do with the bet, since it hadn't been made at that point."

"Then why?" Lily demanded furiously. Leaping from her seat, she trod closer. But not close enough that he could touch her.

Fletcher wished she didn't look so hurt, so betrayed. Knowing she wasn't going to take this next part well, either, he stayed where he was with his legs braced apart and arms folded in front of him. "I made a promise to your grandmother Rose that I would look out for you and keep you from getting involved with some guy who'd break your heart," he told her in a low, gravelly voice.

Lily smirked, a mixture of bitterness and disbelief lacing her expression. "But that didn't include you?" she guessed contemptuously.

"Actually," Fletcher said, forcing himself to be completely honest even as he tracked the moisture glimmering in her eyes, "I was exactly the kind of guy I thought you should stay away from."

Lily shook her head, as if that would clear it. "Which is why she went to you? Because it takes one to know one?"

He matched the biting sarcasm in her tone, knowing he had earned every bit of it. "I think that may have been the general thinking. She seemed to figure I knew the score, and since she had developed a rapport with me because I took care of your family cat, she must have felt she could trust me to do what she'd asked.''

Lily threw up her hands and began to pace, her slender hips swaying gently beneath the delicate fabric of her dress. "And you just said yes?"

Fletcher shrugged helplessly. "She was on her deathbed, Lily. She needed, wanted, peace of mind."

Lily sat there, letting it all sink in, not knowing whether to erupt in bitter laughter or break out in gut-wrenching tears. So she did a little of both—simultaneously. "So what did you win when I refused to go out with Carson and went out with you instead?" she asked as she brushed her fingertips beneath her eyes.

"Nothing."

She glared at Fletcher, painfully aware that if not for the promise he had made to her grandmother Rose that he never would have felt beholden to stop her from going after Carson McRue or gotten so involved with her in the first place.

"I know guys," Lily said in a low choked voice. "They always wager something." She struggled to keep her composure even as she took another step closer, tilted her face up to his and demanded coolly, "What did you get if I rejected Carson McRue in favor of your swaggering attentions?"

Fletcher's golden-brown eyes gleamed with a mixture of displeasure and regret. "A hundred bucks."

Lily studied him as the words sunk in, feeling all the more devastated. Somehow she couldn't see him spending that much time and energy on her for that little payoff. Even if he had made a promise to Grandmother Rose. ''That's all?'' she echoed contemptuously.

Fletcher compressed his lips together grimly and admitted reluctantly, ''From each one.''

Now they were getting somewhere. ''So if you lost it was going to cost you five hundred dollars. No wonder you went all out,'' Lily concluded sardonically as she turned her back and paced away from him.

If only she hadn't. Lily blushed hotly as she recalled how foolish she had been, letting her guard down so completely. How much better it would have been, she decided morosely, if she had given up her dream of experiencing passion and excitement and remained the Ice Princess of Holly Springs. She pivoted back to him with as much dignity as she could muster, trying to forget she had ever been so wildly in love and lust with him, she had done things she'd never thought possible—such as playfully tying him to the bed, and doing a provocative striptease.

Never mind that she'd revealed her most private thoughts and wishes and fears! Allowed herself to be truly and completely vulnerable with him. Shame flooded her from head to toe. ''Get out!'' She pushed the words through lips that felt frozen.

He held out his hands and came toward her imploringly. ''Lily—''

''I mean it, Fletcher.'' Her voice was shrill, angry, unforgiving as she shoved him out of her physical space. ''Get. Out.''

His jaw hardened at the implacable tone in her low

voice. "We're not through here," he warned determinedly.

"Oh, yes, we are," Lily shot back as she rushed past him toward the foyer. She stared right through him as she opened the door and held it wide. "I never ever want to see or hear from you again."

"SO WHAT'S THIS I HEAR about there being trouble between you and Lily?" Fletcher's mother said when he arrived at the church Sunday afternoon, well in advance of the ceremony.

In the chapel, he could see the photographer taking pictures of Janey in her wedding dress. She was a beautiful bride. Glowing with happiness. Just as Lily would and should have been if he hadn't screwed up so badly.

"I don't know what you're talking about," Fletcher said, flushing guiltily.

Helen Hart grabbed him by the elbow and steered him into the currently unused church nursery. She shut the door behind them, looking every bit the practical disciplinarian and loving mother of six that he remembered from his youth.

"Fletcher Matthew Hart."

Oh, no, here it came. The use of his full given name.

Fletcher winced.

"Don't even think about trying to shut down on me now," Helen continued.

"Now I really don't know what you're talking about," Fletcher replied stubbornly, casting yet another warning look at his mother.

Helen paused, obviously struggling to find a way to reach him. "I wish I could say you weren't always this way," she told him gently, all the love she felt for him in her eyes. "But the truth is you've always taken everything to heart."

Fletcher blew out a weary breath. He didn't want to be rude, but he didn't want to discuss this like some brokenhearted fool, either, even if that was exactly what he was. "Come on, Mom," he reminded gruffly. "I'm as cynical as they come. Everyone knows that."

"Hmm." Helen looked him up and down, her dissent with his assertion obvious. Reminding Fletcher that if anyone knew how vulnerable he was deep down, it was his mother.

His devil-may-care bravado worked on everyone but her. She'd held him when he cried as a kid. She'd tried to comfort him when he'd felt lost and alone— and refused to admit it—as an adolescent and an adult. For all the good it did either of them. Fletcher had remained unable to let his guard down completely with anyone but Lily. And now, because of his reprehensible, ungentlemanly behavior toward her, Lily had turned away from him, too.

His mother paused, still trying to figure out how to get him to confide in her and let her help him with his troubles. Finally, she said, in that soft, tender voice that always tore him up inside, "I've been trying to figure out how you got so cynical, Fletcher." Regret scored her expression. "What I did—or maybe didn't do when you were growing up—that made you this way."

"You didn't do anything," Fletcher declared impatiently.

"Then why don't you feel you deserve to be loved, heart and soul? Why won't you fight for it the way you fight for everything else? Fletcher, I've seen you work over an animal that everyone else has given up on. I've seen your confidence, your determination, when it comes to healing. I just don't understand why it doesn't carry over into your personal life. Unless…" She paused, bit her lip, then turned to him, as stubborn in her love for him as ever. "We've never talked about this. At the time, you wouldn't let me. And I felt maybe it was for the best to let it go and move on, forget that it had ever happened, rather than make it a regret you'd have to carry the rest of your life. But now I wonder if my attempt not to burden you that way really weighed you down even more."

Fletcher knew what she was talking about, even before she said, "You may not recall this, but your last one-on-one outing with your father didn't go particularly well."

Fletcher only wished he had been able to forget that evening. He had carried the burden of that unsuccessful heart-to-heart his dad had tried to have with him that night for nigh on twenty years now, not wanting to burden anyone else with his own self-centeredness—especially his mother, who had been so devastated by his father's death.

"He took you out for ice cream because he wanted to have a heart-to-heart with you," Helen continued, trying to jog his memory.

And I acted like he wasn't even there, Fletcher thought, as the failure to be the kind of son he should have been burned like acid in his gut.

Silence stretched out between them. His mother seemed to know she had struck a nerve, and simply waited. Fletcher searched his mother's eyes, almost afraid to ask. "What did Dad say to you about that night?" he demanded gruffly. *Please, tell me he didn't say anything that hurt you, too.*

Helen lifted her slender shoulders in an elegant shrug and kept her eyes firmly locked with his. "The usual. That he was worried you were taking too much upon yourself." Her eyes clouded with self-admonition as she recalled, "You were only ten, but already your father and I both could see you were way too hard on yourself, Fletcher."

"I deserved to be," Fletcher countered contemptuously, rejecting the forgiveness she was offering. "Lest you forget, my actions led directly to the death of our family's dog." A sin for which he would always pay.

Helen's expression was maternal as she reached out and touched his arm. "People make mistakes, Fletcher. We all do. What separates the grown-ups from the perpetual adolescents is the ability to forgive yourself, make amends to those you have hurt and move on."

And what if you couldn't do that? Fletcher wondered as he turned away from the compassion in his mother's touch. What if your actions had been too hurtful?

Fletcher felt his eyes begin to burn. "I know you

mean well, Mom," he told her impatiently as he crossed to the window. "But you're way off base here." He blinked, said hoarsely, "You have no idea how stupidly and unforgivably I've behaved this time. Not that that's any surprise, either," he concluded bitterly.

He had a talent for making offhand decisions that somehow evolved into terrible disasters. And for the life of him he couldn't figure out why. It wasn't like he meant to get the family dog killed, or disrespect his father the very last time they saw each other, or crush every single one of Lily Madsen's heroic illusions about him and stomp all over her heart. But he had. And there was not going to be any recovery from this catastrophe, either.

Helen caught his arm, forced him to face her. "You are not unlovable, Fletcher, although to my considerable ongoing frustration, I know you have often deemed yourself to be." She paused, looking him up and down with the keen-eyed awareness only a mother had.

"Just tell me what happened between you and Lily," Helen implored again.

Fletcher had never been inclined to confide his deepest thoughts and feelings in anyone—save Lily. Now, she was gone. And heaven knew he needed to talk to someone. So, in halting words, Fletcher finally bared his soul to his mother and told her what he had done. "So you see," Fletcher concluded with disparagement, "Lily's grandmother Rose should never have asked me to look out for Lily. I was the absolutely wrong person for the job."

"Has it ever occurred to you," Helen asked with the patience of a saint, "that maybe there was a reason Rose did that?"

Fletcher threw up his hands in frustration. He didn't have a clue where his mother was going with this.

"It takes one to know one? And since she wanted to keep Lily away from guys who would hurt her—"

"That is not why Rose chose you," Helen interrupted sternly.

"Then why did she?" Fletcher demanded right back, mocking her highly exasperated tone.

"Probably because she saw the potential in pairing you—you, who are far too cynical and self-deprecating—with Lily, who up to now has been far too naive and idealistic. Being together has obviously helped both of you."

Had, Fletcher thought. Past tense.

"And it could help you even more if you'd just put aside this cynicism once and for all and go after what you want, which is of course the woman you love."

"I never said I loved Lily," Fletcher stated.

Helen smiled with the wisdom gained by rearing six children into adulthood. "You don't have to. It's all over your face whenever you look at her or see her." Helen clamped a reassuring hand on his shoulder. "Even a fool could see that."

"Lily doesn't."

"Oh, Fletcher, haven't I taught you and your siblings anything? It is from adversity that strength is born. Painful as it was, your father's death forced us all to grow, to love, to be there for one another through thick and thin.'' She angled her head at him. ''And we've done that, haven't we?''

The lump was back in his throat, big time, as he thought about how much his family meant to him. Gruffly, Fletcher looked at his mother and acknowledged, ''You know we have.''

''Well, Lily's had a lot of sadness in her life, too. But she deserves love, too.''

Like he didn't know that? Like he didn't want to be the one to give it to her? Fletcher raked both his hands through his hair. He felt as if the starched collar and bowtie were suffocating him every bit as much as this conversation. ''Did you miss the part where I completely blew it with her, Mom?''

''If you want to win Lily's hand in marriage, then go and do it. Because I'll tell you, Fletcher, I've seen the way she looks at you, and you've already won her heart.''

Had he? His heart said yes. His cynical side told him that Lily never would forgive him, and she'd be right not to given the way he had behaved. His mother was still looking at him, waiting for that miracle to happen. Fletcher grimaced as frustration welled up inside him once again. ''Easier said than done, given the fact she won't even talk to me.''

Helen pooh-poohed that considerable obstacle with a wave of her hand. ''No success in life is ever final—nor is any failure.''

''ARE YOU GOING to be able to walk down the aisle on Fletcher's arm?'' Janey asked Lily as she and the other bridesmaids gathered in the anteroom at the back of the church. "Given the fact that you pretty much hate his guts right now? Because if you can't, we can switch the members of the wedding party around. Try to configure it some other way."

Heaven knew Lily was tempted to do just that. Every time she even thought of Fletcher, never mind caught a glimpse of him, it was all she could do not to burst into tears. She had loved him so much! Given him so much. Only to be betrayed and humiliated in the most awful way.

"There's no question he made a fool of me," Lily muttered as she attempted to apply her mascara with a hand that was not cooperating.

Emma and Janey exchanged concerned looks as Lily paused to remove the smudge of mascara she had just left under her right eye.

Since they were both ecstatically in love with the men of their dreams, they wanted everyone to be equally happy.

"From what Joe told me about the wager, it was just Fletcher trying to put a spin on his attempts to protect you from Carson McRue," Emma said.

"Yeah, well, there was a reason for that, too." Briefly, Lily explained about the secret promise he had made to Grandmother Rose. So she'd either been a mercy date or a means to an end. Neither option appealed to her.

Fletcher's cousin Susan said, "For what it's worth, I've spent a lot of time with Fletcher since we grew up. He puts on a show, pretending he's the tough guy. And until you and Spartacus came along, his heart was in lockdown,'' Susan acknowledged seriously. "But once he started spending time with you, once he began to open up, he changed. To the point, I don't think there is any going back. And isn't that what true love is all about? Finding someone who helps you confront your own personal demons, whatever they are, and be the best person you're capable of being?''

"What are you trying to get at?'' Lily demanded.

Susan leaned closer to the mirror as she reapplied her lipstick. "I don't think you should keep punishing him for a mistake he made before he really got to know you. It isn't as if he doesn't know he did wrong—he does. It's just that he can't take it back.''

Emma, who had made her own share of mistakes in her romance with Joe, nodded. "Sometimes you just have to move on, Lily.''

Janey agreed. "Otherwise you end up like Cal and Ashley.''

"What's going on with them, anyway?'' Lily asked. The two had only been married a short time when Ashley took off for a two-year fellowship in Hawaii, leaving Cal to practice sports medicine and orthopedic surgery at Holly Springs Medical Center. Both doctors insisted there was nothing wrong with their marriage, they were simply pursuing their careers to the best of their ability. But no one in town really believed it, including their own families. It was as if something had happened to drive them apart before Ashley left, and the rift was only getting wider.

Janey shrugged. "Nothing good, I can tell you that."

"Which is why we want you and Fletcher to be together," Susan explained as Emma helped Janey adjust the tiara in her hair. "Because true love—like what you share with Fletcher—might only come once. So you shouldn't let it go."

"How can you still be so idealistic?" Lily asked in frustration, wanting to believe there was still a chance for her and Fletcher, but not sure she should.

"When my own marriage ended in divorce?" Susan asked.

Lily nodded. She never would have said it, but now the assertion was out there.

Susan's expression turned reflective. She, too, had been scarred by a parent's death and knew what it was to grieve for all the times lost, the things not said or done. "I guess it's the romantic in me," Susan shrugged finally. "All I know is that when I saw Fletcher come into Wild Girls Only and take you out of there—there was something in the way he looked at you…so fiercely tender. Lily, I'd give anything if someone looked at me like that. My ex—Perry—never did."

The door opened and Helen Hart walked in, looking resplendent in her mother-of-the-bride dress. Janey took one look at her mother's face and knew, as did everyone in the room, that there was a glitch in the wedding. "What is it?" Janey asked her mother anxiously.

"Your brother Dylan isn't here yet."

Lily looked at the clock on the wall. "And the wedding starts in a little over an hour." Oh, dear…

Emma studied her mother-in-law with knowing eyes. "It gets worse, doesn't it?" Emma guessed with a wedding planner's aplomb.

Helen nodded. "He called Hannah Reid to pick him up at the Raleigh-Durham airport."

Lily had been wondering why the mechanic and part-time chauffeur, generally known to be perfectly on time, was so late arriving at the church. "So we're missing a bridesmaid and a groomsman," Lily concluded.

Helen sighed and looked all the more troubled. "Right."

Janey muttered something unladylike. "I'm going to kill that little brother of mine. Why did he have to wait until the very last minute to fly home for this? Wasn't it enough he missed the rehearsal and dinner last night?"

"Don't shoot the messenger—" Joe popped his head in, then seeing everyone was decent, strolled on in "—but Cal asked me to deliver the bad news to everyone."

The tension in the room increased tenfold.

"Let me guess," Janey said wearily as she found a seat. "His wife, Ashley, isn't coming?"

Joe shrugged his broad, hockey player shoulders. "Problems getting away. I guess that OB/GYN fellowship she's doing in Honolulu is pretty demanding." He walked over to lace his arm around Emma and give her a husbandly kiss.

"How's Cal taking it?" Susan asked.

"Not good." Joe's frown deepened. "He's outside on the cell phone, having words with his wife about her no-show right now. He's absolutely furious that she waited until the very last minute to give him the news."

"Oh, dear," Helen said as she collapsed next to the bride on the worn velvet settee. She fanned herself. "What else could possibly happen?" she asked in mother-of-the-bride distress.

"That's what I'd like to know," Janey muttered.

And then someone else was at the door to the anteroom. They all looked up. Fletcher was standing there. Tall, imposing. And more coolly determined than Lily had ever seen him.

Fletcher looked straight at Lily. "I want a word with you," he said. "Right now."

Lily's heart thundered in her chest as her spirits rose and crashed and rose again. She couldn't believe he was throwing down the gauntlet like this, right there in front of everyone. "This isn't the time," she murmured haughtily.

"It's exactly the time—" Fletcher drawled, crossing swiftly to her side.

When she resisted, he simply tucked a hand beneath her knees and swept her up into his arms, cradling her against the hardness of his chest.

"—since the nuptials are probably going to have to be delayed due to the late arrival of my younger brother."

"Remind me to thank Dylan when I see him," Lily muttered, excitement climbing into her cheeks.

Fletcher carried her past the approving expressions

of the other members of the wedding party, out the door and up the stairs that flanked either side of the vestibule.

"The only one you're going to be thanking is me," Fletcher said as he continued past the door to the balcony, where the organist and soloist were warming up, down a narrow hallway, to an open doorway.

"Why would I be thanking you?" Lily demanded, trying hard not to inhale the intoxicatingly masculine fragrance of his cologne and skin as Fletcher strode into the supply closet, switched on the overhead light and shut the door behind them.

He set her down gently and raked her with a glance that brought forth a wealth of memories, both tender and erotic. "For refusing to give up on us."

The room—already small—got smaller, more intimate yet.

"What?" Lily prodded, stubbornly ignoring the tingles of desire he was creating, just being near her. She reminded herself that although she had given him her whole heart and soul, he had never once said he loved her. "Your brothers haven't paid up yet?"

Refusing to react to her needling, he gave her a look that said she was making this unnecessarily hard on them both. "I paid them."

That was news. Lily blinked, struggling to understand why he would have done such a thing, when he had clearly won his wager. Unless…? "I'm going out with Carson McRue?"

Fletcher scoffed and gave her that you-are-my-woman-look again. "Only when hell freezes over."

"Then why did you pay them?" Lily asked, trying not to warm at the fiercely possessive expression on his face.

He caught her hand and tugged her close. "To make a point."

She still didn't get it. "Well, it's completely escaping me," she said, mocking his droll tone to a T.

He wrapped both arms around her, and held her tenderly, looking deep into her eyes. "That my chasing you and courting you and protecting you was never about the promise or the wager, it was about what I was already feeling deep inside and was afraid to admit. It was about the fact that I love you," he said in a rough voice laced with all the affection she had ever wanted, and more. "Do you hear me, Lily? I. Love. You. Fletcher Hart loves Lily Madsen."

She looked into his eyes and knew he meant it, every word. And suddenly the mistakes they'd both made, the errors in judgment—and there had been plenty on both their parts—were negligible. Tears of happiness flooded her eyes. Knowing at last all her dreams were coming true, she rose on tiptoe, laced her arms around his neck and kissed him soundly. Once, twice, three times. When at last they drew apart, she felt peace in her heart unlike anything she had ever felt.

He lifted a hopeful brow, still holding her as if he never wanted to let her go. "I take it that kiss means you love me, too?" The smile on his face said he already knew the answer.

"With everything I have and am," Lily affirmed contentedly as their hearts beat in lovely harmony.

He smoothed a hand down her spine, bringing her closer yet. "Then marry me, Lily," he urged in a low voice, thick with emotion. "So we can spend the rest of our lives together."

Letting her actions speak for what was in her heart, Lily rose on tiptoe once again and kissed him again, even more passionately this time. Fletcher kissed her back. "Is that a yes?" he whispered as her whole world went right again.

"Most definitely," Lily replied, her heart pounding as she drew back to look him square in the face. "But only on one condition," she stipulated firmly.

"Anything," Fletcher told her, looking ready to make all her dreams come true, and then some. Not just for now, but for the next fifty, sixty years. "You just name it."

Lily grinned, aware she had never felt so happy—except for maybe when they'd made love and he'd shown her without a doubt all the woman she could be. She pressed a cautioning fingertip to his lips. "You have to swear to me you'll never make another bet concerning us with anyone but me."

To her delight, he didn't even have to think about it. "Done," he pledged firmly.

The happiness inside her bubbled up, lighter and more buoyant than ever. "And you have to promise me you will win this next one."

Interest flickered in his eyes at the possibility of another bet—this one made with her. "You need victory, Lily?" he promised cheerfully, kissing first her hand, then the inside of her wrist. "I'm your man."

"Good. 'Cause this is it." Lily wreathed one arm

about his neck, smoothed her other palm over his chest. "I'm betting the two of us will last forever."

"Sweetheart," Fletcher said, taking her back into his arms, for another long, slow, incredibly tender and possessive kiss, "that's a wager we're destined to win."

* * * * *

In August 2004,
Harlequin American Romance presents
PLAIN JANE'S SECRET LIFE,

the fourth installment in
Cathy Gillen Thacker's charming
miniseries
THE BRIDES OF HOLLY SPRINGS

*Weddings are serious business in the
picturesque town of Holly Springs!
Everyone knows the grandiose Wedding
Inn is quite a sight to behold in this neck
of the woods. The inn is owned and
operated by matriarch Helen Hart, the
no-nonsense steel magnolia who has also
single-handedly raised five macho sons
and one feisty daughter. Now all that's
left is getting all her headstrong offspring
to march down the wedding aisle!*

*In this new tale, dashing groomsman
Dylan Hart is in the doghouse because
he's late to his own sister's wedding....
Watch those sparks fly when feisty
chauffeur/bridesmaid Hannah Reid takes
it upon herself to* personally *escort him
to the ceremony!*

*Turn the page for a sneak preview of
PLAIN JANE'S SECRET LIFE....*

Chapter One

Unbelievable, Hannah Reid muttered to herself as she watched Dylan Hart saunter out of the Raleigh-Durham airport terminal, full entourage in tow. His sister Janey's wedding was in less than an hour, and the handsome TV sportscaster was stopping to sign autographs and shake hands. Okay, so the autographs were for beaming kids, the handshakes for their parents and the two airport security men walking beside Dylan. But still, Hannah fumed, as Dylan scanned the pick-up area, finally broke away and strode quickly over to the Classic Car Auto Repair van she had idling at the pick-up.

"Where's the Bentley?" Dylan asked as he opened the rear door and climbed inside.

Irked he was treating her more like a chauffeur who was there to cater to his every whim, than an old family friend, Hannah pulled out into the traffic exiting the airport. The least he could have done was issue a personal greeting. *If not climb in the front and ride shotgun beside her.* "Back in Holly Springs. It's being used to transport the bride and groom to and from the ceremony. Speaking of which—"

"Yeah, yeah, I know, I'm running late," Dylan acknowledged cheerfully. "But so, from the looks of things, are you. Unless you *plan* to participate in the nuptials with grease on your face?"

Hannah touched her hand to her cheek and then rubbed her soiled fingertips on the leg of her denim overalls. Damn. She couldn't believe she had done that again....

"Not to worry." Dylan caught Hannah's eye in the rearview mirror and winked. "I won't tell anyone where you've been."

"Har de har har." With effort, Hannah kept her eyes on the road. She did not need to be noticing how much more handsome Dylan Hart seemed to get every time she saw him. Just because he was super-well put together—even today he had traveled in a sleekly attractive business suit and tie—and looked mouthwateringly handsome on the television screen, did not mean she had to go all gaga over him, too. So what if he had bedroom eyes, a mesmerizing sexy smile and dimples cute enough to make her sigh out loud. Or expertly cut, soft and clean sandy brown hair, glowing golden skin and crinkly laugh lines at the corners of his eyes? He also had the exceedingly stubborn Hart jaw—and the personality that went with it. Plus a way of standing back and merely observing—rather than indulging in—life, which she found extremely irritating.

"Where have you been?" Dylan continued conversationally as he moved around in the back seat, giving her repeated glimpses of his broad shoulders and sturdy compact body in the rearview mirror.

"Emergency call, working on a vintage Jag," Hannah muttered over the rustle of clothing being pulled out of a carry-on garment bag. One of his masculine, nicely manicured hands accidentally brushed the side of her face. *What was he doing back there?*

More rustling as Dylan sat back slightly and shrugged out of his suit jacket and tie. "Today?"

Hannah knew what he was thinking—she was in this wedding, too. "I had time," Hannah said defensively as Dylan pulled a shaver out of an expensive leather toiletries bag and began running it over his jaw. "Or I thought I did." She spoke above the buzzing noise of the razor and scowled. "Until your flight was late." Now they were all off schedule. And she would have even less time to put herself together, before walking down the aisle—on Dylan Hart's arm!

"Weather delay." Dylan shrugged as he slapped on some deliciously sexy aftershave. He moved his head toward the window and peered out at the afternoon sky. "Looks like it's clearing up here, though."

"Finally." Hannah sighed in relief, as she took the turnoff to Holly Springs. "After days of rain."

Was it her imagination or was she hearing him undress? "Do you have your seat belt on?" she asked with a frown, telling herself what she was imagining could not be so.

Dylan chuckled and continued to move around behind her on the vinyl seat, much more freely than he should have. "Ah—not at the moment, no."

He sounded distracted.

So was she.

Aware her heartbeat was accelerating and her imagination was soaring even more wildly out of control, Hannah gripped the steering wheel even tighter. She tried not to think about the way her skin had tingled when he had accidentally brushed her face. "We're on the highway, Dylan!" Hannah reminded primly.

Safety, however, seemed the least of his concerns. Dylan moved around all the more. Out of her peripheral vision, Hannah saw the shirt he had been wearing whip past the back of Hannah's head and the starched white tuxedo shirt come off its hanger.

"I trust your driving—you having a chauffeur's license and all," Dylan replied lazily, the hard, sexy muscles of his chest flexing as he worked his way into the required shirt in the confined space.

Oh, my. Was it getting hot in here or what?

Hannah reached for the AC controls, and turned it to Maximum Cool as beads of perspiration gathered between her breasts. "Even so—" Hannah reprimanded as she heard another, even more telling, zip and whoosh of cloth moving over skin.

"I can't exactly get my pants off with my lap belt fastened," Dylan drawled.

He had to be teasing her. He would not actually be stripping down all the way, not in her vehicle. Right...?

Hannah glanced over her shoulder, sure she would find she had been imagining things. Instead, her eyes widened at the long muscular legs, the sinewy chest, visible through the unbuttoned halves of his crisp white shirt and the sexy lines of his broad, muscular shoulders. At six foot even, Dylan Hart might be the shortest in stature of the five Hart brothers, but there was *nothing* small about him.

Hurriedly Hannah turned her gaze back to the road. Her palms were trembling. Her emotions ran riot. ''What are you doing?'' Hannah demanded in a strangled voice, trying without success not to remember the rest of what she had seen. Black silk bikini briefs. Clinging to…

Never mind what the fabric was molding!

She had a job to do here—and that was to get them both to Janey and Thad's wedding!

Coming soon from

HARLEQUIN®

AMERICAN *Romance*®

Cowboys BY THE DOZEN!

by Tina Leonard

The Jefferson brothers of Malfunction Junction, Texas, know how to lasso a lady's heart—and then let it go without a ruckus.

But these twelve rowdy ranchers are in for a ride of their lives when the local ladies begin rounding up hearts and domesticating cowboys...by the dozen.

Meet cowboys number five and six in

FANNIN'S FLAME
HAR #1018
available May 2004

and

NAVARRO OR NOT
HAR #1037
available October 2004

And don't miss Calhoun's story coming in December 2004 and Archer's story coming in February 2005!

Available at your favorite retail outlet.
Only from Harlequin Books!

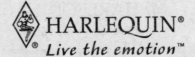
HARLEQUIN®
Live the emotion™

Visit us at www.eHarlequin.com

HARCBD

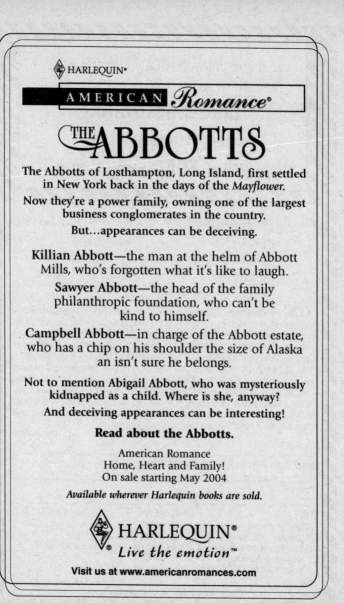

If you enjoyed what you just read,
then we've got an offer you can't resist!

Take 2 bestselling
love stories FREE!
Plus get a FREE surprise gift!

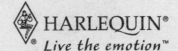